REAL ARTISTS HAVE DAY JOBS

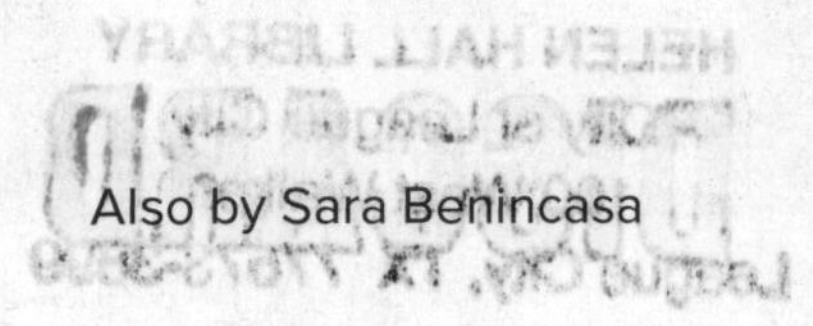

Also by Sara Benincasa

Agorafabulous!: Dispatches from My Bedroom

Great: A Novel

DC Trip: A Novel

REAL ARTISTS HAVE DAY JOBS

(AND OTHER **AWESOME THINGS** THEY DON'T TEACH YOU IN SCHOOL)

SARA BENINCASA

WILLIAM MORROW
An Imprint of HarperCollins*Publishers*

The essays “Real Artists Have Day Jobs,” “Do It Anyway,” and “It Gets Better, Mostly” appeared in earlier forms on Medium.com.

The essay “It Gets Better, Mostly” appeared in an earlier form in *Internazionale* magazine.

The essay “Stop Apologizing for Everything” appeared in an earlier form on Jezebel.com.

HarperCollins books may be purchased for educational, business, or sales promotional use. For information please e-mail the Special Markets Department at SPsales@harpercollins.com.

FIRST EDITION

Designed by Diahann Sturge

Library of Congress Cataloging-in-Publication Data has been applied for.

ISBN 978-0-06-236981-9

16 17 18 19 20 OV/RRD 10 9 8 7 6 5 4 3 2 1

To my brother, Steven Donnelly,

and his new wife, Elaine Powell Donnelly,

I wish you many years of happiness and wacky hijinks

CONTENTS

Contents

THERE ARE 52 ESSAYS IN **THIS** BOOK BUT **PLEASE** READ **THIS** PART FIRST

Before we begin, it behooves me to provide an accounting of my lack of qualifications to write this book.

I am an author and comedian. I have a master's degree in teaching grades seven through twelve from Teachers College at Columbia University. I have an undergraduate degree in creative writing from Warren Wilson College. I am a licensed driver in the state of New Jersey. I think I got certified for CPR a couple of times but I've totally forgotten how to do it. I don't even remember the Heimlich maneuver.

I have no degree or certification in medicine, psychology, psychiatry, counseling, social work, fitness, nutrition, health, massage therapy, acupuncture, craniosacral therapy, Thai yoga therapy, equine therapy, canine therapy, avian therapy, Reiki (which was "invented" in 1922 by a Japanese dude and appeals to the Orientalist sensibilities inherent in American culture, even and especially among white liberals seeking a panacea to the admittedly restrictive and damaging tenets of conventional religion, so, enjoy paying for that), scrimshaw, or homeopathy (which is also not real, sorry).

Lest you think me entirely without fondness for the woo-woo-ooky-spooky in this life: I play with friggin' fairy cards designed by Brian Froud. I've gotten Reiki (for *free*) because sometimes it's just nice to be still and have somebody focus on you—like when girls would play with each other's hair at middle school slumber parties. I do enjoy spiritual practices. I do see the beauty in various religions. I do hope there is Something Else Out There, and that it is good and right and loving and tolerant of our occasional recreational drug use—the Big Cool Stepmom in the Sky.

I also enjoy science, and if the vast majesty of the natural world is truly all there is, I'm okay with that. I think that's pretty damn beautiful.

I have always been suspicious of those who give advice without admitting their own misdeeds and missteps. To me, the most authentic insight comes from those who acknowledge their own shortcomings and readily admit they are still working on improving themselves each and every day.

I used to write an advice column for a website that eventually just stopped responding to my emails. I mostly enjoyed my time there, particularly because the advice I gave was born of my own mistakes. I never purported to be an expert or a holier-than-thou preacher; I felt this would be disingenuous. Anyway, after I was ghosted out of a gig there, I thought it might be interesting to try to write a series of fifty-two essays (one for each week in the year, if you so desire) about life as an adult human who is just trying to be a better and happier person. An alternate title for this book might be *I'm Not Perfect, You're Not Perfect, Let's Work on It While Drinking Iced Tea and/or Bourbon.*

This is a book of advice and ideas inspired by my thirty-five years of flaws, fuckups, failures, and occasional good choices. It is written with love and enthusiasm and excitement and nervousness and fear and pain and all of those important human emotions. I hope it makes you feel less lonely. I hope it makes you think. I hope it makes you smile. I hope it makes you confident. I hope it makes you buy my other books, all at full retail price.

And I hope it makes you laugh.

Sara Benincasa
Los Angeles, CA
December 2015

Chapter 1

REAL ARTISTS HAVE **DAY** JOBS

Have you ever dreamed of being a *real* artist?

Have you ever wondered what it would be like to call yourself a *real* painter, or a *real* writer, or a *real* actress, or a *real* musician?

Have you ever described yourself as someone who does something amazing and magical and wonderful and life affirming and then added "on the side"?

Well, you might not like what I have to say.

Because I have come here today to deliver the unfortunate truth that you are lying to yourself.

You are not going to become a *real* artist one day.

You are a real artist right now.

You are a real artist when you sit in traffic, when you wait for the dentist, when you clean up the toys in your kid's bedroom.

I have known I was a real writer since I was a little kid in Flemington, New Jersey.

How did I know I was a writer?

I got lucky.

A grown-up told me.

When you are a little kid and an adult tells you that you are something, you are wont to believe it. Remember this the next time a kid tells you she is a ballerina, or a math genius, or a comet streaking through an inky black night sky.

For years, I wrote only in my journals. I wrote diary entries, and sometimes stories about myself or other people I knew or celebrities or imaginary creatures. When I stayed home sick from school, I took pieces of yellow stationery with the Mack trucks logo (this was where my grandma worked) and I wrote and drew comic strips about magical people.

In the third grade I wrote a short story called "Jared's Christmas," which won an award from the New Jersey Council of Teachers of English. There was a ceremony and I was very, very nervous, because even then I had panic disorder, but I accepted my award and got my certificate and my mother and father clapped really loud and it felt really good to know I was a real writer.

I was a real writer then, and I am a real writer now. The only difference is that sometimes people pay me to write things, and more people read these things than read "Jared's Christmas."

These days, I am allegedly a grown-up. While I don't know you personally, I know that you are a real artist if you can answer "yes" to any or all of these questions:

Do you make art?

Do you make art because something inside you tells you that you *must* make art?

Do you make art because it's the only way you can feel like yourself sometimes?

Do you make art because it brings you joy, and also pain, but the good kind of pain, the kind you need in order to remember that you are a real person with worth and value and power and all of the feelings (yes, even the shitty ones)?

Do you make art because it's fun?

Would you make art regardless of whether anybody paid you to make art?

Do you stay up at night after the kids have gone to sleep, when you really ought to be in bed yourself, or at least doing laundry, just because it gives you a few precious minutes to make art?

Do you sit at your computer in your office and make plans to use the money from your office-and-computer job to buy supplies to make art?

Do you make art that some people love?

Do you make art that some people hate?

Do you make art that some people ignore?

Then congratzel tov, my friend. *You* are a real artist.

When I was twenty-three, I decided to become a high school teacher in order to support myself as a writer. And so I taught high school in the Southwest and no one published anything I wrote, though I tried to convince them it was a good idea.

I was a real writer then.

I was also a real writer when I was an assistant working at a law firm specializing in immigration for fashion models (truly, the Lord's work). I was a real writer when I worked at a company in the South Bronx, in a neighborhood so violent we were required to sign out of work no later than 4 P.M. so that we could reach the subway before nightfall (rumor had it there had been an assault and a murder a few years back, so the company was cautious). I was a real writer when I worked at a fancy pet boutique on the Upper East Side, where customers spent upwards of three hundred dollars on luxurious cat beds, and eccentric women came into the shop pushing puppies in prams. I was a real writer when I worked at Planned Parenthood. I was a real writer when I hosted and produced a satellite radio talk show about sex and love and dating five nights a week from 8 to 11 Eastern, 5 to 8 Pacific. I was a real writer when the show got canceled and I collected unemployment. I was a real writer when I worked at a start-up and I was a real writer when I quit the start-up to write full-time.

I am a real writer now, and I will be a real writer until I die, whether or not I always do this as my full-time job. I have had day jobs in the past and I have no reason to believe I will not have day jobs in the future.

The biggest myth we are fed as artists is that we need to sustain ourselves solely on our art. This is ridiculous. Every artist has at some point in time had some other job. Some of them kept these jobs their entire lives. In the latter category: William Carlos Williams was a doctor in New Jersey; Henry Darger was a custodian in Chicago; Harvey Pekar was a VA hospital clerk in Cleveland.

In more temporary capacities: Maya Angelou was a cable-car conductor; Sandra Cisneros was an administrative assistant; J. K. Rowling was a secretary; Jeremy Renner was a makeup artist. (Please read that again: *Jeremy Renner was a makeup artist.*)

Art does not require an MFA. Art does not require a BA. Art does not require a high school diploma. Art does not require any formal education at all.

Art does not need your full-time attention. Art does not

demand that you starve in order to afford paint and canvas and brushes, or knitting needles and yarn, or a chain saw for your badass ice sculptures, or whatever your tools may be for your particular medium.

There is more nobility in hard work than in pure luck (though every artist can use a bit of that). You'll make better art after a day at the office than you will after a lifetime in an ivory tower.

Real artists have day jobs, and night jobs, and afternoon jobs. Real artists make things other than art, and then they make time to make art because art is screaming to get out from inside them. Screaming, or begging, or gently whispering.

Don't ever let them tell you you're not a success. Don't ever let them tell you you're not good enough. Don't ever let them tell you you're not the real deal.

More important: don't ever tell yourself any of these things.

Believe me when I tell you that no matter how much time you spend at the office, it's just a side gig.

You are an artist, full-time, twenty-four hours a day, seven days a week.

Now go make your art.

Chapter 2

HOW TO READ A BOOK

I'm not what you might call an avid reader.

It's a shameful admission. But my literary habits were not always so deficient. I used to be downright bookish. As a child, I was a voracious reader. Saddled as I was with a wild younger brother of my own, I adored the Fudge books by Judy Blume. I never much liked babysitting or being babysat, but I loved the Baby-Sitters Club series by Ann M. Martin. The Sweet Valley High series, created by Francine Pascal (*not* Francine Prose, as I would remind myself frequently), was pure aspirational candy fluff. I was bowled over by the idea of two gorgeous, identical blond twins living in so exotic a locale as Southern California. I didn't know that when Pascal created the series, she had never actually been to California. I simply took her account of life in that mysterious kingdom to be fact.

Anything by L. M. Montgomery was marvelous to me. Attempting to nurture a fondness for Canadian literature, my cousins in Toronto saw to it that I also read the Bruno and Boots books by Gordon Korman. Years later, at the *Los Angeles Times*

Festival of Books, when our panels were scheduled back to back, I ran up to him and said, "Gordon Korman. I am Sara Benincasa. I am a writer, too, and I love your books." Then I ran away, like a normal person does.

When I was a kid, I liked stories about kids who did secret things away from the prying eyes of adults. I liked stories about kids who had private adventures.

And so it isn't surprising that one book in particular captured my imagination beyond all others. I love it so much, in fact, that when I recently moderated a panel discussion about comedy and memoir at the Brooklyn Book Festival, I was excited to answer an audience member's question about our favorite childhood books. I knew the audience, numbering four hundred strong on the steps of Brooklyn Borough Hall, was vastly more interested in hearing from panelists Bob Saget and John Leguizamo than from me, but I couldn't contain my enthusiasm.

"*From the Mixed-Up Files of Mrs. Basil E. Frankweiler* by E. L. Konigsburg is the *best*!" I blurted out.

This drew a round of applause from the audience of New Yorkers. Because *From the Mixed-Up Files of Mrs. Basil E. Frankweiler* is nothing if not a celebration of New York City.

I encourage anyone to read this marvelous little adventure story, but in case you haven't got the time, here's a synopsis: Octogenarian millionaire widow Mrs. Basil E. Frankweiler narrates a tale of two very extraordinary children. They don't have magical powers and they don't command armies like children in a popular book might today. They are simply smart, cunning, witty, and determined.

Claudia Kincaid, age twelve, is sick and tired of her regimented, orderly, odiously pleasant life as a child of privilege in Greenwich, Connecticut. She is convinced that her parents don't appreciate her, particularly as they make her do chores that aren't required of her precocious nine-year-old brother, Jamie, or her other brother (Claudia is the eldest of four; the youngest is still a baby). She enlists Jamie, her favorite sibling, to run away from home with her. She chooses him because he's smart, but mostly because he has money—more than twenty dollars, which probably was quite a lot of cash for a nine-year-old kid in the 1960s, even in Greenwich.

The two hatch and execute a near-flawless plan to live in The Metropolitan Museum of Art. They are aided by the general cluelessness of the security staff and by the ready availability of reasonably priced food from Horn & Hardart's Automat. And there's a gorgeous fountain in the Met that just so happens to provide a tidy income for the kids, thanks to the penny wishes of various museum-goers. While living at the museum, Claudia and Jamie become entangled in an art world mystery about the origin of a marble statue of an angel. It's rumored to be the work of Michelangelo, but no one knows for sure. They discover that the statue was sold at auction for just $225 by a Mrs. Basil E. Frankweiler, and they decide to get to the bottom of things.

I lived in New Jersey, about an hour and fifteen minutes away from The Metropolitan Museum of Art. It was my absolute favorite museum in the world (well, of the handful I'd visited in my short life), and when I read Konigsburg's love letter to the museum, I was bowled over. It was the first time I can recall feeling that sense of recognition that sometimes seizes a person when she experiences art: *I see me*. Sometimes art takes us to faraway places, and sometimes it elevates our ordinary school field trips to the realm of the extraordinary. Of course, it helped that I, too, had a brother three years my junior; that I lived not too far from New York City; and that I sometimes chafed at my parents' high expectations. (I'm not sure what eight-year-old actually enjoys obeying her parents, but I felt quite injured by some of their fascist rules—for example, their declaration that I couldn't read under the covers with a flashlight.) In Claudia Kincaid, I found a kindred spirit. In Mrs. Frankweiler, I found an imaginary confidante, a sympathetic listener to whom I, too, would undoubtedly tell all the details of my own schemes and dreams. Of course, unlike Claudia, I rarely actually carried out these schemes.

There was a rather long gap between my elementary school love affair with books and the moment when my high school social studies teacher, Miss Peck, gave me a book by the artist and author SARK (Susan Ariel Rainbow Kennedy) as a graduation present. I loved the bright colors in SARK's world, and I was fascinated by the idea that an author could (or would want to) actually handwrite her own book. You'll note I have not attempted the same feat here, as my own handwriting is atrocious. But SARK knew how to write and she knew how to draw and she knew how to present a truly lovely series of inspirational books that spoke to the touchy-feely hippie flower child in me.

When I was twenty-one, I had a nervous breakdown and dropped out of college. I used to sleep in my bed at home with my books. They felt like guardians. I couldn't control my thoughts or the ceaseless drumbeat of suicidal ideation, but I could control what I fed my brain. I chose to feed it good things, comforting things, reliable things: books, books, and more books. Mrs. Basil E. Frankweiler was there. So was SARK. So were poems by

Rumi, a new favorite book called *Full Catastrophe Living* by Jon Kabat-Zinn, *When Things Fall Apart* by the Buddhist nun Pema Chodron, and any other book that seemed to gaze at me from my bookshelf with a welcoming, steady, nurturing focus. My books accepted me for who I was. They made no comment on my disheveled, sickly appearance as I began the bumpy road back to proper hygiene and age-appropriate behavior. They weren't annoyed or bemused when I rocked myself to sleep, listening to the baby lullaby of a wind-up stuffed giraffe I'd had since I was a baby. They didn't cast aspersions on my new regimen of medication and talk therapy. They were, simply, there for me, as I was for them.

That I grew up to write books is no surprise—I'd dreamed of being a writer since I was a little kid, caught up in affection for Judy Blume and Ann M. Martin and all the rest. But somewhere along the way—perhaps because I spent so much time online—I lost my attention span for long books. Or maybe reading just began to seem less magical, except on very rare occasions, such as when I read Neil Gaiman's *Sandman* comics series. That definitely brought the magic back, at least for a little while.

Today I read books in fits and starts and bits and pieces. I still love reading. I just don't do it all the time. But I've learned to love this less-devoted approach. I prefer serialization, just as I did when I was a kid with Sweet Valley High and the Baby-Sitters Club. And so I break everything into manageable pieces.

This is how I'm reading the books on my Shelf of Good, where I curate a selection of inspiring books: *Yes Please* by Amy Poehler; *Bad Feminist* by Roxane Gay; *Not That Kind of Girl* by Lena Dunham; *Dangerous Angels* by Francesca Lia Block; *Science . . . for Her!* by Megan Amram; and some of that Rumi poetry I enjoy so much. I intend to add *The House on Mango Street* by Sandra Cisneros as soon as my copy arrives.

Little by little. Page by page. Sentence by sentence. Word by word. It's how I write my own books now.

When I read, I count the moments, not the pages. I still surround myself with books like talismans, like magical protectors, like saints. Their mere presence comforts me, encourages me, inspires me.

Perhaps this book will do the same for you.

I certainly hope so.

Chapter 3

EVERYTHING IS INTERSECTIONAL

The first time I heard the term "intersectional feminism," I tensed up. I had no idea what it meant. I was in graduate school to become a high school teacher, and I was used to hearing all kinds of opaque academic jargon thrown around by people who seemed to have a lot of theories and not a lot of common sense. Many of them had gone to fancier, more prestigious undergraduate colleges and high schools than I had. I always wanted to hear practical, real-world examples of how all this highfalutin language could be applied to helping our kids learn more and be happier, healthier people.

"What the hell is 'intersectional feminism'?" I said.

I got a complex explanation involving references to books I'd never read, college courses I'd never taken, and conferences I'd never attended.

"Can somebody put that into words I can understand?" I said to my classmates. "Humor me. I'm from New Jersey."

"It just means recognizing that all forms of oppression are

interrelated," somebody said. "Feminism isn't separate from racism, or classism, or ageism, or any other prejudiced mind-set."

"See, that makes sense to me," I said. "Thank you."

The term "intersectionality" comes to us from Kimberlé Crenshaw, who began using the term in the late eighties to describe what happens when different influences intersect. Intersectional feminism understands that feminism does not just exist to benefit white, wealthy cis women. Nor does feminism just exist for women who've gone to college, women who date men, women who've had children, women who are married, and so on and so forth. I could get into the jargon and the complexities of the issues contained therein, but as we've seen, I like to keep things simple and clear. Plus, why would I wade into those waters when you can read bell hooks or Judith Butler or any one of a number of amazing writers? They've already covered it far more brilliantly than I could.

The main point is this: You've got to recognize that no one in this world stands alone and apart from anyone else. Everything affects everything else. We are all interconnected and interrelated. This isn't some mystical idea (although I love mystical ideas) and this isn't some dry academic concept (okay, I don't love dry academic concepts). This is real life.

Imagine we're on the bus together, and I've got a terrible cold. If I don't cover my mouth with my arm when I cough, I may transmit the cold to you, the unfortunate human sitting beside me. And then you may go home and give the cold to your child, who then brings it to another kid at day care. And maybe *that* kid is immune-compromised, and she ends up in the hospital, racking up bills that her parents can't possibly pay. This creates stress on the marriage and requires the mother to take on a second job, which in turn requires the father to . . . well, you can keep inventing more and more events to add to that chain.

Now imagine the cold is a belief, like the idea that women don't deserve equal pay, or the idea that black people are mentally inferior to whites. Maybe it isn't as simple as passing on a virus, but you can certainly transmit an idea to a child. And that child can grow up and make decisions based on that idea. This person's sexism or racism will have a kind of domino effect that will not only affect the people in his life, but the people in those people's lives, and on and on and on.

This is why activists will often say that activism begins with you. It starts with the little decisions you make every day—the words you choose, the companies you support, the ways in which you invest your time and money.

Look, I'm not the self-actualized queen of intersectional harmony. I'm a self-centered, privileged white chick with more degrees than she needs. I've gotten plenty of shots in this life, some because of how hard I've worked, some because of luck, and some because America tends to hand a lot of shots to people who look like me and come from a background like mine. It does not hurt me one bit to examine my own privilege and the ways in which I deliberately and inadvertently participate in systems of oppression.

People on both sides of the political aisle talk disparagingly about "liberal white guilt." I'm liberal and I'm white, but I don't feel guilty. I feel responsible. I feel motivated. I feel energized. To me, there's a difference between a sense of guilt and a sense of awareness. Guilt wastes everybody's time. Awareness is the first step toward change.

I'm not going to save the world. I'm not *trying* to save the world. I'm trying to be less of an asshole. I'm trying to be a better human being, because it helps other people and because it makes me happier and healthier. I'm figuring it out as I go along, and I'm fucking up and failing and doing well and succeeding. I don't expect anybody to pat me on the head and say, "Good job!" I still haven't read all those fancy books, or learned all the multisyllabic jargon that's currently in fashion. But I'm grappling with the ideas, and I'm trying. I bet you are, too.

Let's make an agreement to try to be a little bit better each and every day, in word and deed and action. Don't be like me and automatically reject a concept just because you don't feel like making room for it in your cluttered brain. You can do it. That's the great thing about brains: they can encompass infinite ideas and infinite possibilities—even the possibility that, one day in the future, we can all love each other and take care of each other. It won't happen in my lifetime, but that's no reason I can't keep reaching for it.

Chapter 4

IT GETS BETTER, MOSTLY

It's early. I'm nervous. I'm waiting out the morning rush hour so I can drive to high school. It's not my high school. I'm thirty-three. It's been ten years since I taught high school and fifteen years since I attended high school. I'm going to a high school to talk about mental illness, which is a thing that I have. I'm going to an AP psychology class.

I check my outfit. I ask my boyfriend if it looks okay. He says yes. I don't want to look like the hippie art teacher but I also don't want to look like the old chick who's trying too hard to be hip. I wear black skinny jeans (I am not skinny—they are XL—extra weight from the drugs, but I'm used to that now), a blue-and-white-striped button-down top, a red belt, and red cowboy boots. These boots are like my security blanket. I wear them whenever I travel, and the airport security workers always compliment them. This happens everywhere—at Newark, at JFK, at LaGuardia, at LAX, at Burbank. You know, everywhere.

I guess most people don't wear red cowboy boots to the airport.

It strikes me that most people probably don't wear red cowboy boots to give a presentation at a high school AP psychology class. I wonder if I should change them.

No. They are my security blanket. I will keep them on.

I take a deep breath. I check the bathroom once, twice, three times. I know that if I check it three times, everything will be fine. Everything will go well that day. I look at myself in the mirror. I make eye contact.

"I love you," I say. If I don't do this, the day will go badly. If I do do this, the day will go fine. I have to do this every time I look in the mirror, or something bad might happen. Will happen. Or something good won't happen. I'm not sure which. I've never been sure which. I just know that I have to do it.

I remind myself: If the kids don't like me, or if I say something stupid, or if (God forbid) I panic, I get to leave. My friends are still my friends. They don't go to high school anymore.

I AM FOURTEEN. I am crying in the front office at the school. This is the Lower House front office, in the building where freshmen and sophomores dwell. It's a big public school, two thousand kids. The biggest in the county. I am crying.

I am not sure why I am crying, except that I can't stop. I am late to school because I was crying and couldn't stop.

The secretary looks at me sympathetically.

"Maybe you'd better talk to Mrs. Smith," she says. Mrs. Smith is the school guidance counselor.

"No," I say through heaving tears and snot. "I'm okay."

"Well, ask her to sign your pass anyway," the secretary says. Very tricksy, that secretary.

I nod. I am obedient. I am the class vice president. I get A's, mostly. I am on the flag squad, even though that is dorky and embarrassing; I still manage to be reasonably popular. I'm funny. I wear a lot of J.Crew, which is what you wear at my high school.

I like to figure out how to talk to certain people and invent a language and catchphrases of our own, inside jokes that bond us together. I make a lot of eye contact. I listen well.

I do what I think will please other people.

I smile and nod again and I go into the counselor's office.

She says the hall pass can wait for a minute. She says we can talk.

I stare at my boots and blink three times. This is a thing that I do to make sure everything is fine.

She shuts the door.

I AM SIXTEEN. The pediatrician says I can take the drug for the panic attacks and the depression. He says it will help. I look at the pills uncertainly and decide I will never, ever, ever tell anyone about this. I thank him for his help.

My dad says maybe I'll just take them for a little while, just to get me through this rough patch. The pediatrician says a lot of times this disappears when someone gets older.

"Does it really get better?" I ask him.

"Yes," he says.

I cannot wait to get older.

I AM TWENTY-ONE. I have not left the house in days, or maybe weeks. I still take the drug every day.

The drug is not working.

I am afraid to use the bathroom. I am afraid to eat. I am afraid to leave my bedroom. I live alone, thank God. *Thank God.*

My bed is my safe space. I lie in bed all day when I am supposed to be at class. I constantly think, *I want to die. I want to die. I want to die.* This does not concern me. It is a constant drumbeat in my head, and you can get used to a constant drumbeat, the same way you get used to that dripping sound in your bathroom or the endless barking of your neighbor's dog.

But lately it has changed a little. *I want to die* has been replaced, sometimes, with *I want to kill myself.* And this is a different thing entirely. Death can be passive; something one receives; a gift or curse from illness or accident or simple old age. But killing oneself is active. It is a choice. It is something I can do, and I might do it, because the pills don't work and I'm tired of pretending that I am still class vice president, good-natured, and funny, always with the inside jokes and the eye contact.

I haven't been eating. I haven't been bathing. I am skinny and stinky. My friends don't hear from me anymore.

I still drink water. I get it from the sink in my studio apartment. The sink is in my bedroom, along with the mini-fridge and the hot plate. And because I still have water, I have to go to the bathroom. Only I am afraid to go to the bathroom, because I'm afraid to leave the bedroom, or the bed, except to drink water. I can't tell you why I am afraid, except that I know that if I go to the bathroom, if I do anything outside the bedroom, something bad will happen.

I grab a bowl. I squat over it in my bed, and I urinate. Most of the urine makes it into the bowl.

I put the bowl under my bed. I'll dump it in the sink later, when I have energy. I don't have a lot of energy these days.

I go to sleep. It is 3 P.M. on a Tuesday. I will not wake for twelve hours.

* * *

"LOOK AT THE raisin," the psychiatrist says, and we all do.

"Smell the raisin," the psychiatrist says, and I laugh.

"What's funny?" he asks, not in a mean way.

"I just don't think raisins smell like anything," I say.

"Try it and see," he says.

I am learning to eat again, which apparently entails sniffing fucking raisins in front of a group of similarly broken humans.

I am twenty-two. I take pills every day, but these are different pills from the ones I used to take. They give me a headache and they make it hard to sleep at night, but to my surprise and my parents' delight, they are starting to work. I don't feel like a zombie or anything—I still cry *all* the time—but I cry less. I can think straight. I even want to eat, sort of, sometimes. I drink a lot of smoothies, because the mushy food is like baby food, and I find that comforting.

I never put raisins in my smoothies.

I never put raisins in anything.

Raisins are gross.

But I oblige people. I do things for them.

I sniff the raisin.

"I guess it smells like a raisin," I say.

"Put the raisin in your mouth, but don't chew," he tells us. "Roll it around on your tongue. Feel the texture. Rub it against the roof of your mouth with your tongue."

This is seriously the dumbest thing I have ever done, and I have done a lot of dumb things.

He tells us to think about all the people who worked to bring us this raisin: the people who planted the grapes, the people who harvested the grapes, the people who dehydrated the grapes (or whatever the fuck they do to make raisins—I kind of zone out for a few seconds here), the people who brought the grapes to market. And so on and so forth.

I get it. The food chain. Circle of life, and all that. We are not isolated. And I think we ought to realize that whatever we consume, it's a choice—a choice that affects other people's lives. I like what he's trying to teach us. I don't like raisins, but I like thinking about how interconnected we all are, and how I'm part of a big web of humanity strung together by love, or whatever it says in the self-help books I am reading as fast as I used to read my college assignments. I live at home and I don't have a job yet so I've got plenty of time to read and meditate and do yoga and think about raisins. My mom drove me here today because I'm still not good with getting out of the house and into cars, but I didn't have a panic attack in the car this time. I practice every day walking to the end of the driveway, holding my parents' hands. Tomorrow we're going to the grocery store. I know I can do it.

I am lucky. I know I am lucky.

I AM BETTER, mostly, for a long time.

I go to a new school. I go to graduate school. I become, of all things, a stand-up comedian.

It's amazing what years of medication and cognitive behavioral therapy can do for somebody. I still have to talk myself out of the house on many days, but I've become used to it.

I write a book. The book is about high school and college and the raisins and other things.

I always wanted to write a book.

I still take the drug every day. It's the New Drug until it isn't.

The No Longer New Drug works.

It works for years.

It works great.

Until it doesn't.

I AM THIRTY-ONE. I am sobbing uncontrollably in a conference room at work. The conference room has glass walls, so everybody who passes can see me sobbing.

It's a start-up office. The start-up is about books. It's fun to work there. I do stand-up at night and wait for The Book to come out, and in the meantime I earn money writing about books at the book start-up. It's pretty great.

On Thursday nights we have wine hour, which means a couple of hours, which also means cocktails, and fresh-baked bread and fancy cheese and whatever else anybody feels like bringing in. It's an open floor plan in a big loft space on Eighteenth Street in Manhattan. The people are nice. The programmers play video games on the big screen on Thursday nights.

It is not Thursday night. It is Monday morning. I can't blame the crying on it being Monday.

"I think I need some help," I tell my boss.

"The best thing about being a freelancer," he says, "is that you get to make your own hours. Choose your own workload. And take care of yourself as best you can. Go home. Do whatever you need to do. You let me know when you can work, and how much you want to work. I want you to be healthy first."

My boss is great. He's really great. I leave for the day, closing the door to the office behind me. I look at it to make sure it's really shut. It looks shut. Is it really shut? I hope it's really shut.

I walk downstairs. The sound of my boots clacks in the stair-well.

I call my parents in New Jersey.

"I think I need to come home for a while," I say. "It's happening again."

"We're coming for you," they say, and they do.

I'm lucky to have them. I'm aware it is a privilege to have a family that wants to take care of you; that is able to come and save you (again); that isn't ashamed of your condition; and that encourages you to get better. I know I'm lucky. I'm so very, very lucky. Which is why it's particularly shameful that I want to die, again.

MY PSYCHOLOGIST SAYS I'm bipolar. My psychiatrist says no way. I have major depressive disorder and I have panic disorder and I have agoraphobia. My psychiatrist has excellent hair and a medical degree. I decide to go with what the psychiatrist says, because it's what all the other psychiatrists have said over the years.

My psychiatrist with the excellent hair has a subspecialty in fertility issues, which do not apply to me because I've determined I will never pass these genes on to another human being. Also, I'd probably have to taper off the meds or at least go on a low dose if I got knocked up and kept it. That does not seem like a viable option—tapering off the meds, or keeping it.

My psychiatrist wants to add a drug.

"It's like a booster for the antidepressant," she says. "In low doses, it helps it work better."

This new drug has a nice name and nice television advertisements. It is an atypical antipsychotic, but my psychiatrist says not to get hung up on that. It will help.

It does help.

I gain weight, but it helps.

I go back to work.

I AM THIRTY-THREE.

The high school that is not mine is three thousand miles away from the book start-up.

I live on the other coast now. Someone wanted to make The Book into a TV show, and I thought that was a good idea, so I came out here to write a TV pilot, and another book, and then another book, and soon I will start writing a fourth book (which will, as it happens, become the very book you are reading right this second). I travel to speak at colleges about my brain and what happens in it, because I think maybe this will help the kids feel better about their brains and what happens in them. Also, I get paid to do this, which is very nice.

I am not getting paid for the high school thing. The high school thing is a favor for a friend. I am not scared of college students but I am scared of high school students.

I have a boyfriend. I have a puppy. And thanks in large part to the atypical antipsychotic with the nice name, I have about thirty-five extra pounds on my stomach, thighs, and butt. I stare at it in the mirror sometimes, right before I make eye contact and say, "I love you."

I pull up outside the high school and I park. This is a huge high school, twice the size of my own.

I go inside. I talk to the secretary in the front office. I get a hall pass. Kids are milling about everywhere. I am terrified, but only slightly.

I use the bathroom.

I go to the right classroom.

I look at thirty unfamiliar faces. They don't look evil. I take comfort in that.

A kid tells me he really likes my boots. I say thank you.

And then I talk. I talk for forty-five minutes. I talk about everything but the peeing in bowls; I figure I can leave that part out. The kids ask questions, good questions. I give answers, good answers. Honest answers (except for not telling them about the pee).

I tell the kids that I'm crazy, but in a good way, and that crazy doesn't have to mean what you think it means, and that you can reclaim that word and make it your own.

There is no shame in crazy.

There is only shame in pretending that everything is okay.

Everything is not okay. And that's okay.

The kids ask more questions.

When we're done, they applaud. It's nice.

I give a copy of Book No. 1 to the teacher. She says she'll read it. I hope she likes it.

Class lets out. I exhale slowly. I did it.

The kid who liked the boots stays after. He comes up to me with tears in his eyes. He twists his hands together. He is beautiful.

"Does it really get better?" he whispers.

"Mostly," I say, and then we talk for a long while.

Chapter 5

DO **IT** ANYWAY

I am bad at a lot of things. I am, in fact, bad at most things. Here is a brief list of just a few of the things at which I am bad:

1. Brushing my teeth (I do it enough, but my technique is all wrong)
2. Flossing my teeth (I always cut myself up)
3. Singing (I have no rhythm, no range, and no ear for music)
4. Cooking (I burn things)
5. Walking my dog (She walks me, really)
6. Drawing (I have no ability to render something pretty)
7. Painting (See "Drawing")
8. Managing my money (It all disappears into books and dog treats somehow)
9. Managing my time (I leave assignments till the last minute)
10. Understanding sports (I call hockey "puckball")

11. Relationships (HAHAHAHAHAHAHAHA, oh, we do have fun)

However, even though I am bad at all these things, I do them anyway. Really! Not necessarily professionally or anything (though I don't see how I'd be a professional tooth-brusher, unless I were my own dental hygienist, which sounds like an actual living nightmare).

When I was growing up, I thought, *Nothing is worth doing unless you can do it perfectly.* This is a stupid bullshit devil thing to think and/or believe. I now say, "Nothing is worth doing unless you can do it *mostly okay.*"

I recently got a puppy. I am historically bad at keeping plants alive, so one would think I could not handle a puppy. It turns out, I can! Mostly! I found people who were good at having puppies and asked them to teach me things about having puppies. I also read things about having puppies. And as it turns out, I am not entirely awful at having a puppy! I am mostly okay at it. The puppy doesn't give a fuck. The puppy leads a life of joy. Her dog walker recently told me that she has a good soul, and you know dog walkers know their shit.

When you are raised to be perfect and then you inevitably turn out to be so very imperfect, it is tempting to stress out over every little thing in life. The fear of failure can emotionally cripple you to the point that you do not attempt anything cool or fun or great. You lead a life that is small and unhappy, or smaller and unhappier than it would be if you attempted something fantastic. And since most of us fail at more things than we succeed at, it seems entirely rational to expect that you would, in fact, fail if you made an actual attempt.

Do it anyway.

Suck at stuff. Fuck up. Fall down. Get rejected. Get shut down. Get passed over. What the fuck else are you doing with your time? Imagining potential failures? Why not turn that potential into a reality? At least you can say you went for it.

Note that I did not say, "At least you can say you tried." As Yoda and my high school color guard coach taught us, there is no "try." You do or do not. You go for it or you don't. You devote yourself to the task at hand or you devote yourself to not devoting yourself to anything.

Here is a true story. I wanted to write a book about my life but I did not know if anyone would read it. So I started telling stories on little stages around the country when I had time off from my work. I pretended I was on vacation, but really I was doing research.

Sometimes five people would come and sometimes fifty people would come. I listened for when people laughed and looked for when people cried and I made notes and I kept those parts in the book proposal, which is the thing you have to make before you sell a book about your life. I did a bunch of other things so that people would (hopefully) pay (mostly) positive attention to me and be interested in this imaginary book I might write.

Eventually I told enough stories and got enough people interested that a company said, "We will publish your book," and I said, "Oh, thank you," and they said, "Now go write it," and I said, "Oh, fuck." Then I wrote it.

It was not a perfect book.

It was not everyone's favorite book.

But I did it! I did it anyway! It was the best feeling in the world, just doing it anyway. I asked for help along the way from friends and writers and my agent and my editor and random strangers, and I cannot emphasize enough how good it is to ask for help from people who give a crap about you. If you think no one gives a crap about you, you are actually wrong. You probably just haven't asked enough people for help yet.

"But what if I ask for help and people say no?" you maybe say to me, quietly.

"DO IT ANYWAY," I definitely say to you, loudly and enthusiastically.

You must tell people exactly what you want from them if you have any hope that they will give it to you. I asked people to review my book (well, my publisher asked them to review my book) in the hope that everyone would love it and write glowing reviews. As it turned out, there were good reviews and bad reviews and okay reviews and great reviews and awful reviews. But. Those good ones and great ones stood out to me, and I never would have gotten them if I had not asked people to read my book in the first place.

Even when you're afraid—especially when you're afraid—you've got to do it anyway.

I had a dream last night that I was standing by as a turtle flushed a toilet (it seemed very normal at the time). The turtle kept pushing on the handle, and the toilet would give one of those halfhearted flushes. I decided I would help the turtle out and I reached over and flushed with enthusiasm. The toilet overflowed and the turtle almost drowned in toilet water and I had to save the turtle from certain shitty death and it was screaming (it could talk, did I mention that?), "I FEEL LIKE I'M BURNING UP!" and the turtle was very stressed out and I felt so, so bad. I was also very afraid I was going to get in trouble for killing the talking turtle with shitty burning toilet water. I fetched the turtle, and it was panicking, and I said to the turtle, "Just breathe. I'll breathe with you." And I breathed in, and so did the turtle. And I breathed out and so did the turtle. And just for a moment, in the midst of the shitty overflowed toilet water, we were calm. That's when I woke up.

What the fuck does that mean? I have no fucking clue. Maybe nothing. Maybe a lot of things. I wasn't even sure if I should put it in this essay, but then I thought to myself, *DO IT ANYWAY.* Did it help achieve some artistic goal? Maybe. Maybe it was a stupid digression that detracted from the main point. Maybe this whole essay is too full of swear words and colloquialisms and dumb sentimental crap that isn't going to help anyone out anyway. Maybe I shouldn't have written it. Maybe I shouldn't publish it.

I'm doing it anyway, because I like it. I hope you do, too.

I send you endless psychic high-fives, the embarrassing kind where you try and miss and then laugh at what a dork you are.

You are definitely a dork. So am I. Isn't it great? The dork in me bows to the dork in you.

Get up. Or sit down. Or curl up in the fetal position. Whatever seems necessary. Consider the thing you really want to do that you have not yet done because you are afraid you would suck at it.

Now go do it anyway.

Chapter 6

PUT YOUR CLUTTER IN **PURGATORY**

As a recovering Catholic, I've always enjoyed the concept of purgatory. I don't even know if it's actually presented as canon to this day or if it's up for debate à la the whole "Han shot first" situation (a vastly thornier discussion), but here's the basic idea: Babies who die before baptism don't go straight to Hell. Nor do they go to Heaven, which makes no sense, because they're fucking babies and are literally incapable of sin, so why the fuck wouldn't they go to Heaven? That's where they fucking *belong*. Anyway, unbaptized babies wait in Purgatory. Maybe they're there forever; maybe they get to go to Heaven once they've proven themselves worthy by, I don't know, shitting themselves in an appropriately heavenly fashion? Also, sometimes people die and their souls are not obviously evil and they are not obviously good. They're in some murky gray area, and God needs some time to decide. Those souls go to Purgatory, too. I'm fuzzy on the exact details, but this is the concept that was conveyed to me in childhood by church, family, and, more important, TV and movies.

Now, when it comes to housekeeping, I'm no angel (see what I did there?!). But I do understand that one key to a happy home is some degree of cleanliness. I'm not a total dirtbag, but I do let things pile up here and there. Okay, everywhere. Not in a hoarding fashion, but in an "I'm too lazy to put that where it belongs" fashion. It is a fact that I will not allow the talented, patient woman who cleans my house twice a month to actually enter my bedroom.

"I can fold clothes if you just tell me where the clean ones are," she will say.

"They're in a pile," I say. "It is indistinguishable from the pile of dirty clothes. I just really don't want to subject you to that. You work too hard already." She does—she's got her own cleaning business, and she's also a newly minted forensic psychologist. She just got her undergraduate degree. After dealing with my home, I am fairly certain a grisly crime scene will be easy.

If I just cleaned my own home like a proper human being, I would not need to pay someone to come in and do it for me. However, I have always been terrible at keeping my house clean. I'll just blame it on my parents without really examining why. Fun! Now let's move on.

One solution I found to my situation was to create a Purgatory Bag. The concept of the Purgatory Bag is quite simple: Once a month, or whenever you feel like it, you go around your house and throw a bunch of clutter in a bag. Not trash, mind you—you throw the trash out. I'm talking about clutter. Knicks and knacks and bibs and bobs and whirligigs and hoodledeedoos. Crap you don't need but aren't quite ready to part with yet.

Then, on a designated day—perhaps it is the first Sunday of every month!—you have a Purgatory Bag session. You go through your most recent Purgatory Bag and decide what goes to Heaven (its proper place in your home or someone else's home) and what goes to Hell (the garbage can). Your Purgatory Bag can be very large or very small or somewhere in between. You can pick different Purgatory Bags for each month! So if in May you feel like dealing with only a few things, you fill a small grocery bag with things and then figure out what you want to keep or give to a friend and what you want to ditch. But maybe in June you're feeling more adventurous, so you grab a big-ass plastic garbage bag and fill it until it's almost too heavy to lift.

The only real rule of the Purgatory Bag is that on the designated day, you empty it completely. Nothing stays in the Purgatory Bag; it either goes to a proper place or gets trashed. If you donate a bunch of stuff to a charity, you can get a receipt for your donation and write it off at tax time. Isn't that delightful?

The Purgatory Bag is a fine innovation for those of us who care enough to do the very least. We've got energy to spend on other things, like saving the dolphins and raising our children or training our pets or raising our children's trained pet dolphins. We're fired up for a climate change protest or a shift at Starbucks or a butt-waxing session (it seriously doesn't hurt as much as you think—I've done it only twice but it was really quite revelatory). The Purgatory Bag means that we *will* clear the clutter—eventually. It's a slow, steady, manageable way to chip away at stuff. And sometimes you forget what's in your Purgatory Bag, so when you go through it, you find some delightful surprises. Be your own Santa! Look at all those half-used lipsticks and random pens! How thrilling! Rock on with your disorganized self. I'm right there with you.

Chapter 7

WHEN YOU DON'T **KNOW** WHAT **TO DO,** ASK A **SUCCESSFUL** WOMAN

When I can't figure out what to do, I ask a chick who is a pro at handling that particular type of situation. If I don't know what the best form of exercise is for me, I inquire of a body-positive, accepting, kick-ass, strong personal trainer of the gal variety. If I don't know how to eat food that isn't made of garbage, I ask a smart lady nutritionist who I know won't sell me some shitty diet pills. If I'm scared about going to a business meeting in sunny Hollywood, I ask a woman who regularly slays business meetings and makes way more money than I've ever seen in my whole life. If I have a broken heart, I ask a tough yet nurturing broad who has survived a divorce or an awful breakup and gone on to be a happier, healthier person with a new partner who is extremely attractive and great at cooking/fucking/cooking and fucking.

I recognize that if you identify as a man, you may be saying, "Hold on there, sister. I am a dude. So I do not relate to this thing you are telling me, because you are assuming I am a woman, and I am not a woman."

Au contraire, mon frère. If you are a dude, this is all the more reason you should follow my advice! In our society, most of the time, women have to work harder than men just to be taken seriously. We work harder to get job interviews. We work harder to earn money. We work harder to manage family and job responsibilities. Some of us grow humans inside our bodies and then push them out or have them surgically removed in a procedure that involves cutting into us and pushing our internal organs aside. Sometimes, in this process, our pussies split a little bit or all the way to our anus (this is true!) and have to be sewn up, all so we can make more people. And if, like me, a gal is fortunate to have the liberty to not choose reproduction, she still usually gets her period until menopause. Do you understand what it's like to bleed out of your most precious and sensitive organs on a regular basis *like that's fucking normal*? Also, I've heard menopause can be awful and sometimes you can't sleep because your body is just so hot and uncomfortable. I plan to drink through it.

Let's also not discount the experiences of ladies who are born in bodies that have parts other than what are considered lady-parts by certain folks. Maybe they do not experience some of the aforementioned physical burdens/blessings of ladydom, but they sure as hell experience other stuff that is tough and strange and complex and difficult and beautiful and amazing. Let's acknowledge, admire, and celebrate the ladies who live in a world that sometimes says, "You are not ladies!" Perhaps these ladies have the toughest time of all. Perhaps not. Everyone's experience is different. My main point is this: the word "lady" encompasses worlds.

Anyway, women are inherently tougher than men. And yeah, we often have to work harder just to get through the day. I love dudes, but let's get real: when you need to get a job done, you should ask a woman who's done it before and done it really, really well.

Sometimes, when I have an entertainment industry question and a Very Successful Woman is not available (Very Successful Women tend to be Very Generous but also Very Busy), I ask myself, "What would Amy Poehler do?" This is an excellent question for actresses, writers, comedians, and other creative types. I don't know Amy Poehler personally and I cannot testify to her character, although I have heard nothing but positive feedback from my friends who've ever been fortunate enough to work with her. But even if Amy Poehler were an asshole, I would still ask myself, "What would Amy Poehler do?" Because when I look at her career trajectory, I say to myself, "Yes. Yes, indeed." I shall explain why in this helpful list.

1. Amy Poehler has written for television. I would like to write for television.
2. Amy Poehler has *created* television shows. I would like to create television shows.
3. Amy Poehler is generally regarded with enormous respect within the comedy community. She is very talented, of course, but also she works her fucking ass off and everybody knows it. I would like to be regarded with enormous respect by my community, not just for talent (many people have this!) but moreover for a great work ethic (not as many people have this!).

4. Amy Poehler has a bunch of money that she earned by working hard. I would like to have a bunch of money that I earned by working hard.
5. Amy Poehler does amazing things to elevate the position of girls and women in the workplace. I would like to do amazing things to elevate the position of girls and women in the workplace.
6. Amy Poehler probably owns a well-constructed house (I don't know if this is true, but it seems likely). I would like to own a well-constructed house.
7. Amy Poehler is a boss. I want to be a boss.

I'm in Los Angeles right now, going to meetings and trying to develop a project with some really amazing folks. I call it my Convincing Men to Give Me Money Tour, which is really a misnomer because working in this business means you're always trying to convince somebody to give you money (usually it's men, but sometimes it's women and that's very exciting). So my professional life is really a constant process of convincing somebody (usually a man) to write me a check so I can make something weird and funny.

Anyway.

In one of these meetings, somebody said, "Ooh, Amy Poehler would be great for this."

At this point I said, "You mean *this* Amy Poehler?" and pulled Amy's book, *Yes Please,* out of my giant bag. Then I pointed to her picture on the cover and I grinned.

"Well, I guess we know what your opinion is on that!" they said.

I realize in retrospect that was kind of weird, and also that writing this chapter may be kind of weird. You know, when you really admire someone, you don't want them to get the idea that you're a creepo. But I find that in my own life, when somebody comes up to me at a book signing or a party or a show or whatever and says, "I don't mean to be a creepo, but I really dig your work," I always get excited and say, "You're not a creepo! That is really kind and makes me happy!" Sometimes you have to get rid of the idea that you've got to be cool and ironic and sarcastic and detached all the time. Sometimes you just have to be a real dork and admit that you think somebody is the tops. It'll probably delight them, so long as you're polite and kind.

Now, your mission is to find your own personal Amy Poehler in your own industry and ask yourself what this very successful woman would do. If you want to write a novel, it is perfectly fine to ask yourself, "What would Roxane Gay do?" Roxane Gay is excellent at writing novels and also books of essays! She is probably better than you are at writing novels and also books of essays! And she's sold a ton of them and won much acclaim for her work. So look at her choices in life and just copy them as best you can.

If you want to be a boss at a big company, ask yourself, "What would Sheryl Sandberg do?" The answer, of course, is lean the fuck in. But beyond that, what would she do? In fact, what *has* she done? What kind of education did she seek out? What sorts of jobs did she have along the way?

If you want to be a schoolteacher, think of the best lady schoolteacher you ever had. You might even want to write her a letter and ask her for advice. She'll probably be tickled to death, because unlike movie stars and famous novelists and celebrity executives, most schoolteachers don't get a whole lot of credit for their awesomeness.

Now listen to me very carefully, because this part is extremely important: Do *not* ask, "How'd you get that?" I cannot tell you how many times I've been asked "How'd you get that?" about a book deal or a TV gig or a spot on a comedy show or any number of neat things for which I worked really really really really fucking hard. I know plenty of people—mostly women—who get asked this question on the regular, and it pisses almost all of us off. "How'd you get that?" sounds so incredibly insulting. It conveys the message that you think there's some easy route to get whatever it is you want, and, moreover, that you expect somebody to just *give you the secret formula*. I usually give one of two answers:

1. "Well, I was born, studied very hard in school, worked really hard to get good grades and do lots of activities, had a nervous breakdown in college that left me suicidal, did an enormous amount of psychological work in order to get to a place where I could leave my room and eventually my home, went to a new college, struggled with depression and anxiety some more, ended up in the emergency room, got out of the emergency room, failed half my final semester, worked really fucking hard in an insane high school in the AmeriCorps program for shit money, finally got my undergraduate degree, immediately went to graduate school in New York on a bunch of loans I'm still paying back, student-taught in the public

schools, realized I didn't want to be a high school teacher, graduated from grad school, worked a bunch of weird jobs at all hours of the day so that I could do comedy at night, started blogging for free, started making videos for free, did a shitload of stuff for free to prove that I could do it for pay, started getting paid but still did a ton of stuff for free, gladly eschewed an active social life for many years in order to get what I wanted, got representation, got more work for more money, kept working my ass off, wrote a book, got really depressed again, got better, worked even harder, wrote a pilot based on the first book, wrote another book, wrote another book, wrote a fourth book, worked with awesome people and with jerks and did my best to be a decent human being along the way, without once ever asking somebody, 'How'd you get that?' as if the answer were pat and simple and as if I deserved to know it in the first place. So, yeah, that's how I 'got that.'"

2. "Oh, LOL, I just sucked a bunch of dicks!"

Instead of the noxious and awful "How'd you get that?" I suggest saying, "I really admire the thing that you did. I would like to do that thing one day but I know it takes a lot of hard work to get to this moment. Where do I even start? Do you have any advice for me? I would be so honored if you did." And then, if the person is kind, she will happily and generously give you some tips. She may even offer to assist you in your quest. I know so many brilliant women who are ready and willing to help as best they can. If you write them letters or email them, they may not be able to respond right away, but they often will respond in some fashion. And if they don't, just remember that they are extremely busy being Boss Ladies and may simply not have the time to get to your question. Imagine they are sending you good and encouraging vibes, and reach out to another successful woman. Eventually, somebody will give you a lovely piece of advice.

And remember—to somebody else out there, *you* are a more successful woman, or dude, or gender-queer person. So if you know somebody looks up to you, you might consider giving a bit of helpful advice yourself on love or sex or work or life or death or origami. You might even realize how far you've actually traveled from your earliest days of striving and fighting. We can't all be Amy Poehler, but we've all got something to give.

Chapter 8

YOU **CAN** DO **MAGIC**

When I was thirteen, I thought I was a witch. Well, *kind of* a witch—I knew witches couldn't really fly or turn cats into dragons or anything like that, but those skills didn't seem particularly useful to me. Flying would probably entail high-altitude travel, which science class taught me was quite cold and uncomfortable unless one were ensconced in a temperature-regulated metal flying device. And as for turning felines into fearsome monsters hell-bent on death and destruction, well, that seemed a bit redundant.

I was pretty sure I was some kind of witch, though not the kind found in fairy tales. I spent a lot of time in the two competing witch stores in New Hope, Pennsylvania. That the New Hope economy can support two witch stores is a testament to the marvelously freaky nature of that particular wee hamlet outside Philadelphia. One of these stores is called Gypsy Heaven, which sounds like and probably is the title of a Stevie Nicks song. The other is called Mystickal Tymes, which sounds like and probably is the title of a Renaissance Faire somewhere in the Midwest. Both are wonderful in their own ways, staffed by knowledgeable actual witch people who probably get tired of enduring awkward jokes from slightly frightened tourists from New Jersey.

I bought incense and decks of tarot cards I'd never actually learn to use. I bought books about being a modern witch, which seemed to mostly entail hanging out with other lady friends in the wood, menstruating in sync while chanting about the Divine Mother. I was pretty sure none of my friends in middle school would be into doing that with me, so I decided I'd have to be a solo practitioner and do this magic thing on my own, in secret.

The most important thing a secret solo home witch must do is build her own altar, and the most important objects on that altar are candles—a pink one for feminine energy and a blue one for masculine energy, or so one of my books said. At that point in time I was but a budding baby feminist, not yet a fully realized Fourth Wave warrior badass who understood and celebrated the fluid nature of gender identity, so this binary notion of magic seemed perfectly acceptable. I would light my candles and say an incantation of some kind and then mix whatever herbs I'd grown out back in our garden. I'd bow to all four directions and send my intention out into the Universe, to the Divine Goddess.

Then I'd wait.

One thing I quickly learned about the Divine Goddess was that she generally didn't respond to requests for boys to ask me out. She also didn't make me any better at math, or at finding my body in space so as to not be the biggest dork in dance class. She didn't make me win baton-twirling competitions. She didn't straighten my hair, shrink my nose, or make me popular.

After a little while, I stopped casting spells. It just seemed pointless to waste time chanting alone in my room when I could be shopping at the Limited Too, looking for that one special outfit that would say to everyone in social studies class that I was cool and beautiful and worthy of love.

I gave up on the blue-and-pink-candle version of magic, but I never quite gave up on magic itself. As I grew older and moved even further away from my Catholic roots, I sought the advice of astrologers and soothsayers and frizzy-haired women with intense eyes who told me they could cleanse me of panic or cure me of my psychic pain. One woman who read my energy told me the reason I didn't enjoy sex was not that I had been raised in a church in which my desires were demonized or that I simply hadn't grown comfortable in my skin yet, but that I had been raped as a child.

"No, that never happened," I said.

"It did," she said. "You just repressed it." Then she tried to charge me three hundred dollars for a special "purification" ritual.

I left and never went back, because fuck that lady and her terrible notions of "impurity." As if a survivor of assault needs to be "fixed" in some way. Also, her gross apartment smelled like soup.

What I realized over time was that magic was whatever I wanted to make it. Like religion, it was whatever anyone wanted to make it. And while I continue to yearn for a loving experience of the Divine Goddess, or the Big Woo, or the Whatever It Is That Is Out There and Loves Us (if such a Thing actually exists), I've taken matters back into my own hands. Only now, I don't worry about blue candles or pink candles or buying the right magic implements.

Here's what I do. It is only what I do, and not what you "should" do or "shouldn't" do. This is what helps me. Maybe it will help you. If it does, great! If it doesn't, that's fine, because as we've established, magic is what *you* make it. Invent your own ritual if mine doesn't work for you.

Sara's Simple 10-Step Magic Ritual

1. Light a candle (not one of those smoky ones, and also make sure it's not near any papers or anything because the last thing you want during your magic ritual is to have to put out some freaking fire, am I right?).
2. Stare at the flame. (Not too close! You don't want to singe your eyelashes! One time I burned my hair by accident and it smelled like ass roasted over the pit of Hell.)
3. Think about a good thing that you want. (Not a bad thing! You must have good intentions. Don't do magic for vengeance. It doesn't work, plus witches say it comes back and bites you in the ass real hard, or something to that effect.)
4. Say out loud, "I want this good thing. I deserve this good thing. I will receive this good thing with love and honor and stuff." (You don't have to add "and stuff" but I find it's quite helpful to cover all my bases.)
5. Smile.
6. Take a deep breath in and exhale slowly. Repeat as often as you like.
7. Bow to the candle.

8. Say "thank you." (No, I don't know to whom you are saying thank you. Maybe it's God. Maybe it's the Universe. Maybe it's yourself, for making the time and the space to do this weird little ritual of love.)
9. Blow out the candle.
10. Get to work.

My magic is easy, fun, and silly by design. I don't charge for it, and I make no promises as to its efficacy, because that's not what magic is about. Magic is about taking the time to check in with yourself, to honor your own needs and desires as valid, and to engage in the ridiculous art of hope.

You can do magic, and you can do it however you want, whenever you want, wherever you want, with or without candles or spoken words or eye of newt (please don't hurt a newt) or Nag Champa incense. Your life is one giant magic spell and you are a fabulous, fantastic witch regardless of gender. Don't ever let anybody tell you otherwise. Blessed fucking be.

Chapter 9

FEEL ALL THE FEELINGS

Many years ago, I slept with a dude. I mean, I've slept with multiple dudes, but I slept with this one dude in particular. I think we slept together two or three times, though I can't really remember it—it was so long ago, and it wasn't a serious thing. I liked him and thought he was cool and funny. Like me, he was a comedian. Unlike me, he didn't have representation, so after he asked, I was happy to put him in touch with my manager at the time. And she kindly gave him some perspective and advice. He wanted to grow his career and, like many comics, felt he deserved more fame and fortune than he'd acquired. That hunger sometimes manifests as entitlement, but I've learned you don't get the prize you don't want. You have to work for it. So I understood. I wanted to help the guy out, not because we slept together, but because he was nice enough and I thought he had good stage presence. His comedy wasn't really my thing, but that's okay. You could see he was personable and that counts for a lot. Sometimes he'd ask me questions about self-promotion or other business things. I did my best to convey what I could, based on my relatively limited experience.

I did not become his girlfriend, because I can't be everybody's girlfriend. Trust me, I've tried. It does not work. I was never going to love this person, but we had fun for a very brief period of time. It wasn't serious. At least, I didn't think it was.

Pretty soon, I started dating people in a more dedicated fashion, and I assume he did, too. I moved on to new things, new experiences, a new life. I spent a couple of years in California, came back to New York to write a book, and finally adjusted to a semi-quasi-bicoastal life more concerned with writing than with performing. I don't know what he did, because we weren't in touch. I might have said hi a couple of times via Facebook or Gchat or something in the early years, the way you might to an old coworker with whom you were friendly. Anyway, by the time of the exciting events outlined in this tale, I hadn't thought about him in a while. I didn't know if he was still doing comedy, because I didn't know anything about him.

Then, out of nowhere, I get this tweet from a nice-seeming stranger who says some folks were talking about me on a show. You've never heard of the show, so don't worry about it. Was it on TV? Was it on the radio? Was it on a podcast? *Who can say?* I am mysterious.

She said the names, and they were folks I used to know (one of them was this dude, another was a friend of his). I was so surprised. It was like hearing somebody say, "Hey, I ran into your high school lacrosse teammate, you remember this guy?"

Then she sends me the clip. And then she says, "Sorry."

Uh-oh.

I shouldn't have played it, but I did.

Some people say they'd love the ability to read minds. Not me. I'd hate it. I don't need to know the awful thoughts some folks have about me, and I don't want them to know the awful thoughts I have about them. If I hear only the nice thoughts, that's only part of the story, so I'd rather stay away from that particular superpower altogether.

Well, turns out I didn't need to use magic to hear what this ex-almost-not-even-a-flame thought of me. Because this guy—the one I slept with a few times six years ago, the one I tried to help out when he wanted career assistance—well, wow. He unloaded about me. He went off. It was pretty freaky, in that it seemed utterly unconnected to anything important. It didn't have to do with the topic at hand. It felt random and cruel.

He said quite a few unsavory things ("insanely untalented" sticks out, but I suppose that's subjective, right? "Manipulative" and "liar" seem a bit harsher) and then concluded with a bizarrely detailed fantasy about my death. I assume he didn't have a boner when he said it, but I can't be sure. Then the other person, whom I used to know a little, a woman whose only characteristic I can recall is a passionate affection for handbags, laughed and laughed and laughed.

Well.

That was quite a way to start my day.

My first reaction was utter confusion. Had I done something to upset these people? I hadn't seen or heard from them in years—I didn't even know they were still trying to get a leg up in the fun game we call "entertainment." And why, for the love of goodness, was this man so mad at me?

I shared it with a friend who said, "Wow. I think it's safe to say this dude caught some feelings and hasn't let go."

My friend Janine Brito, who is a wonderful comedian, said, "Sara, that's just how magic your pussy is."

I mean, yeah. That seems to be the logical and obvious conclusion. (FYI, it is magical and in fact is a portal to another, better dimension, but I can't talk about that right now.) But that didn't make me feel any better.

Have you ever heard of somebody talking trash about you at a party? This was kind of like that, except in front of audiovisual broadcasting equipment. It did not feel great. I'm no stranger to this kind of thing—when you hang out with writers and comedians, sooner or later somebody's going to write about you. I've written about folks and told jokes about folks, so I get it. There's a fellow I slept with a few times who took the opportunity to condescendingly psychoanalyze me at every turn, like I was a tiny bug under a microscope and not a woman who willingly let him put it inside her. Eventually he did a joke about me in his act on television, but he had the gentlemanly sense to disguise my identity. No problem.

But this was my name. This was in public, amplified by media. Sure, it's a nothing show, but still. It is so strange to witness someone with whom you've been physically intimate saying such awful things about you in a public forum. It feels like a violation. I think the worst part was the way he said the things he said—with such disgust, unchecked bitterness, and rage. *Jeez, who hurt him?* I thought, and then slowly came to the realization that—oh shit—it was me. I hadn't meant to hurt him, but somehow, I had. And he was enraged. Still. Six years later.

It was a little scary.

I didn't want to cry. I've always wanted to be that tough girl who doesn't give a fuck what other people think of her. I tend to acquire girlfriends who are tough as nails, who aren't afraid to get into a fight, the kind of chicks who tell you exactly what they think of you. I admire them so much. I watch in wonder as they order exactly what they want at a restaurant without apologizing for substitutions or changes to the menu items. I hold my breath in awe as they delete men's numbers from their phone and then never talk to them again. I keep talking to pretty much everybody who matters to me, ex-boyfriends included. Some are closer than others, and I don't recommend this method to everyone—it isn't always a healthy choice for the parties involved. But I like to see people move on and be happy, even if it stings at first. And I like to move on and be happy, too. But I've got some hard-ass broads in my life who would rather die than be kind to a douchebag who did them wrong, and I have respect for that philosophy, as well.

I considered my options. I do not enjoy having difficult feelings—they can be very uncomfortable, even deeply painful. I was raised to bottle them up and allow them to manifest in other ways—as backaches, headaches, stomachaches, diarrhea, panic attacks. Only then could they be addressed, cared for, soothed, and healed. The physical was so much easier to understand than the emotional.

The most annoying thing about feelings is that they will emerge one way or another, regardless of how hard you try to get rid of them. You can try to drink them away, smoke them away, fuck them away, snort them away, eat them away. You can put a needle in your arm or cut yourself or walk into a bar and punch the first guy who looks at you funny. I don't suggest doing any of these things. I've done a few of them.

They don't work.

Eventually, the levee breaks. Eventually, you feel what you pretended not to feel.

I have spent a long time avoiding feelings and in this particular instance, I decided to try an experiment. What if I just gave myself over to them? What if I put my deadlines and work aside (including this book, for the day) and just let it all out? What would happen?

I was afraid I would lose my mind. I've been on medication to deal with anxiety and depression for many years. Emotions can feel like weapons of self-destruction. Sometimes, when your brain chemistry is off and you've dealt with a bunch of strange things recently and you're in a weak spot, the emotions can get so big and so scary. It can feel like they are drowning you. It can feel like you have no control, no power. It can feel like you're all alone in the middle of a storm on the sea without a lifeboat.

Boy, did I cry.

I cried and I cried and I cried. I'd just been dealing with a family member's surgery and the stress of deadlines and concerns about some friends. And it all kind of came together for me in a giant ball of emotion, which proceeded to explode in the form of tears.

It was the kind of cry that wears you out. You sob and you sob and you sob some more. Your shoulders shake. You get snot everywhere. It's not the most attractive thing in the world, if you're me. I'm from the Claire Danes school of crying, which is to say—when I cry, I fucking go for it. I *commit.* I'm in the shit. I'm a mess. If you're going to bother having human emotions, you may as well go all the way.

I also reached out to some friends to vent. A few of them—the aforementioned tough broads chief among them—said,

"Let's get him. Who is this guy? Let's *end him*." Of course they didn't want to actually murder the fellow, but they felt that perhaps a metaphorical public flogging was in order. You know, the modern version of putting someone in the stocks in the village square. But though it was tempting, I instinctively knew that wasn't the way to go, either. It would just give him attention, which I'm certain he craves because I don't think he gets a whole lot of it.

So I cried until I stopped crying, at which point I had the good sense to email a woman who is very, very smart and gets dragged in the press all the damn time. I asked her what the secret was to dealing with this. Do you take a Xanax? Do you sleep for days? How do you go on?

She told me the only thing to do is to keep doing the work, always. Keep making content. Put art out into the world. Just keep doing it and doing it and doing it.

I also asked a professional publicist I know, who said, "Sara, when you fight back online, it's a pissing contest and everybody gets soaked."

I knew these broads were right.

So I went back to making my art. I finished up another essay in this very book, and I started to write this essay. It took me a while to sort out what I wanted to say, but eventually, I knew what needed to be done, which was not to write out of anger or revenge, but out of a strange sense of peace.

Some people out in the world will not like you. That's okay. They will talk about not liking you. That's okay, too. As long as you keep doing the work you are meant to do, you're good. Because every moment somebody spends talking shit is another moment they've wasted.

When something bad happens, feel all the feelings. It's healthy. This is good work. The only way to get past it is to go through it. Seek the wise and loving counsel of friends and professionals, and know that this too shall pass.

And remember: As the Buddha once said, "Haters can suck it."

Chapter 10

THERE **WILL** BE **SHIT** DAYS

There is the urge with any narrative of overcoming obstacles to make it sound as if happily ever after were a simple thing, as if the princess were perfectly content every day of her life after the prince rescued her from the tower; as if she always woke up with a smile on her face; as if she raised angelic children without any mess or fuss; as if she stayed youthful and lovely and comely and sexy forever and ever; as if she had easy, frequent orgasms and never once sat alone in the bathroom, crying, wondering how the hell she got to this awful place, in this drafty, piece-of-shit castle with a husband who cared more about his hair than her happiness.

We tell stories about ourselves, about the shit we've been through and the fights we've fought, and sometimes we want to tie it up in a neat bow for the listeners. But real endings aren't so neat and clean. And happily ever after only lasts for so long.

I've struggled with mental illness for my entire life, and I talk about it and write about it often. There is a temptation to present myself as "healed" or "cured" or "fine," to peddle the lie that if someone only follows my foolproof five-step plan (I have no such plan, but I could invent one), they'll be happy and healthy for the rest of their days.

The truth is that there will always be shit days. Always. I don't care if you've gone 365 days feeling blissful and glorious; eventually, you will get a flat tire on a busy highway, or catch a case of explosive diarrhea on an airplane, or find yourself strongly tempted to do that bad thing you swore you'd never do again.

Sometimes shit days just happen. And other times they come about because of our own mistakes and missteps. And then there are those days where we can blame ourselves *and* fate/chance in equal measure.

Recently, I got an opportunity to be on a panel at a lovely venue with authors I admire. They're all wildly successful people whose books sell really, really well, and because I would like to one day be a wildly successful person whose books sell really, really well, I thought it would behoove me to accept the invitation. We were to speak about the practice of reinventing classic tales and putting our own spin on them. This is a thing I did recently in a young adult novel, and I was reasonably pleased with the results.

"Sure," I told the publicist. "I'd like to be a part of the panel."

"There will be free ice cream," she added.

"Let me rephrase that," I said. "I would *love* to be a part of the panel."

Bestselling authors, a chance to pontificate on Art™, *and* free ice cream? I was in. I was way in.

I was quite excited up to the day of the panel. And on the day of the panel, I was still quite excited.

And then I screwed up.

I made a series of silly choices that led to a giant panic attack onstage in front of fifty people and the fancy authors and the publicists from my publishing company.

I'm hypoglycemic, which means it's a bit of a struggle to maintain a nice, steady level of sugar in my blood. And when I don't eat properly, I'm wont to go into a hypoglycemic fit of sorts: shaky; heart pounding; sweating; nausea. It feels very much like a panic attack, and sometimes kicks me into an actual panic attack.

Well, I ate practically nothing before the panel. I ignored my condition and thought, "Let me save these calories for the ice cream." This is a bullshit way to think about food and nourishment, but it's exactly the kind of thing we're taught from the cradle—you must deny yourself in order to be worthy of that thing you desire.

If I had eaten lunch and had a good salad with grilled chicken and a nice baked sweet potato, and brought some decent snacks to have on hand (almonds, carrot sticks, an excellent chocolate peanut butter cup, and so on), I would've been ready to rock and roll with that ice cream. And then I could've had a well-balanced dinner afterward and felt fine.

That's not what happened.

Instead, I told myself, "If you deny yourself food all day long, you'll *earn* that ice cream. And then you can have as much of it as you want without feeling bad." I wanted the high of the ice cream, of all that cold sweetness. I thought about it all day long. I don't think I actually rubbed my palms together in anticipatory glee, but it might have happened. I kept so busy with writing all day that I was able to ignore the clear signals of hunger from my body.

Later that evening on the way to the panel, stuck in traffic on FDR Drive on Manhattan's East Side, I couldn't distract myself with writing anymore. I began to feel a bit wobbly. As we sat and sat and sat in that traffic, I began to feel nauseous. My palms tingled, and not in a pleasant way. I wanted to throw up.

"You're fine," I kept saying inside my own head. "You're fine, you're fine, you're fine." And eventually the traffic moved, and we arrived at the destination, and I wobbled out of the car and wobbled into the greenroom, a few minutes before the panel was due to start. I felt victorious. I'd made it! Just under the wire, sure, but I'd made it. I introduced myself to the other authors and congratulated them on their successes in the publishing world, and I suppose I was reasonably charming and pleasant because none of them ran away screaming. I asked someone to procure me an energy bar, and they did, and I tucked it away in my purse for later. After the panel. Because while I was wobbly and shaky and increasingly light-headed, I would surely make it through a forty-five-minute panel, right? Then I could gorge on the energy bar later—ooh, and *ice cream*. I was still hell-bent on earning that ice cream. And if I ate that energy bar, I would've broken my streak of foodlessness. I had made it this far. I was not going to spoil my ice cream celebration with something so prosaic as a helpful combination of protein and sugar, even if it might stave off more of the wobbly feelings.

And then it was time to go onstage.

As soon as I sat on the high director's chair, I knew I was screwed. Just getting up there was an ordeal. Everything seemed to be happening in slow motion. I felt like a lumbering giant, albeit a lumbering giant whose head felt like it might pop off and float away. I stared at the floor and willed myself to breathe slowly and steadily—which probably resulted in great whooshes of air rushing over my lapel microphone.

"Oh no," I thought. "I can't breathe too loudly. I'll embarrass myself."

And that's when I had a panic attack.

I have often described a panic attack as the exact inverse of an orgasm, and I stand by that description. A panic attack often comes with sweat and nausea—I had that taken care of already, thanks to starving myself all damn day. But what makes a panic attack a panic attack is, of course, the titular panic—the giant rush of fear that washes over one's entire body. It isn't rational and it isn't sensible. It's not the sort of thing one can wish away. I've never met a person who was able to snap her fingers and stop a panic attack in its tracks. My preferred method of dealing with the enormous fear is to do my deep breathing exercises and then cry as a release of tension. But I couldn't do the deep breathing, because I was convinced it would sound weird on the mic, and I couldn't cry, because I would traumatize the young readers in the audience (and probably the publicists as well). I wanted to take a Klonopin, which I had in my purse, but I couldn't very well pop a pill in front of all these people. They'd think I was an absolute loon. I already thought I was an absolute loon, and I didn't need them to confirm that belief for me.

Mind you, as I was having all these awful feelings, I was also actively participating in a panel about writing and character development and voice and adapting old stories into new stories and naming one's fandoms (the other writers had cute names for their fans; I think I told the moderator that my admittedly smaller group of fans was known as "geniuses with great taste," though I may just have hallucinated that bit). So I was answering questions as best I could, though sometimes I would forget what we were talking about and have to ask. I'm sure I appeared to be on drugs, when in reality if I'd been on drugs I might have been vastly more lucid and compelling. I did manage to make the audience laugh a few times at my jokes, and that's always a nice feeling.

Finally, I couldn't stand it anymore. I really thought about pulling off the lapel mic and making an announcement: "Hi, everyone! I'm having a great time but I really have to use the facilities! I have poor bladder control, what can I say? Hahaha! See you in fifteen minutes!" And then I could run to the restroom, pop a pill, sob for ten minutes, wash my face for five, and reappear with a confident toss of my head. I was the comedian on the panel anyway; I could probably get away with being eccentric and wacky.

And then I remembered the energy bar.

"Is it weird if I eat?" I said suddenly, probably interrupting someone's very insightful quote about the rise of the reboot in children's literature.

People stared at me.

"I have hypoglycemia and I didn't eat dinner," I said. "I just feel kind of shaky."

At this, the audience smiled understandingly and nodded, seemingly in unison. I should add that we were at a wonderful Jewish community center, and I felt quite fortunate to be in the presence of a community that understands the value of a good nosh. I can't imagine the horrified looks on an audience full of WASPs if I chose to bust out a Clif Bar at the country club or something, but the assembled audience at the 92nd Street Y all but shouted, "Eat, bubbeleh!"

I'm pretty sure I made obnoxious chewing sounds into the microphone, but everyone seemed okay with it. My panic subsided a little, as did my nausea, although both were still present. But I made it through the panel, and gobbled more snacks (plus a Klonopin) during the signing afterward, and then jetted out of there without even eating ice cream. I knew the sugar high from the snacks would only last so long, and I need something more substantial to get me off the sugar roller coaster.

I found a kosher pizza joint and scarfed down a slice. Then I grabbed a taxicab and started crying quietly in the backseat. The pizza and the snacks sloshed around in my stomach; the bright lights of the city swam before my eyes; I went into another panic attack and popped another Klonopin.

In short, it was not my finest day.

I'd like to tell you that I rested in bed that night, grateful for all the good things in my life, and arose the next morning with a look of determination on my face, ready to tackle the day. But the truth is that I slept late and that the panic hangover lasted for another thirty-six hours. I was exhausted by it; I was unable to focus on my work; and I took plenty of extremely lengthy naps in order to avoid asking myself tough questions about why I'd freaked out at the panel. My agoraphobia kicked in and for a couple of days I convinced myself it was better to stay inside most of the time rather than risk having another panic attack. After all, wouldn't it be incredibly demoralizing if I had *another* panic attack in public? Better to cancel a couple of comedy shows and just stay inside where it was safe.

Perhaps it's because I was raised with the Catholic tradition of confession; perhaps it's because I started seeing a social worker when I was a teenager; or perhaps I'm just a chatty

Cathy, but talking about my struggles seems to help. One night, I couldn't sleep (because I'd spent the entire day sleeping, you see) and I remembered how much less alone I'd felt as a younger person when I read other folks' accounts of depression, panic, and agoraphobia. Maybe if I wrote about the shit day, and the ice cream I didn't have, and the authors I felt embarrassed in front of—well, maybe that would help somebody else. And maybe it would help me. If nothing else, it would keep me busy for a half hour. So I blogged about it.

And, as often happens when we share our darkness, I found I wasn't alone. I felt less alone because there were others who totally got what I was saying, who had "overcome" any number of issues—eating disorders, addictions, insidious diseases—and found themselves stumbling backward, messing up, being wildly imperfect. Not being inspiring. Not being magical. Just being gross and real.

It helped to know I was not a freak. Or if I was a freak, I was in abundant, loving company.

Later that week, I started leaving the house again for reasons other than brief dog walks. About five days after the panel, I even went to a party and had a nice time. That felt pretty cool.

No one is perfect. No one is impervious to steps back, to relapses, to regressions. Triumph over one ailment does not mean triumph over all difficulties. You get to be imperfect. You get to be flawed. You get to be human. You get to make poor eating decisions, to forget about self-care, to be cross and grumpy and moody and sad and anything else you want to be. It will almost certainly get better, but first you've got to slog through the day. Whether we say it or not, the rest of us are all down there in the muck with you.

Chapter 11

ELECT YOUR **OWN** EXECUTIVE **BOARD**

Many years ago, I became friends with the writer and comedian Baratunde Thurston, author of *How to Be Black,* a book you must read. Baratunde is known all around the world for being smart and wise and good and funny and handsome, and he works very hard to make the world a better place. He's currently a supervising producer on *The Daily Show with Trevor Noah.* One of the good practices I've picked up from Baratunde is the idea of maintaining a small, close network of geniuses who can provide wisdom and insight into special problems or opportunities that arise in my life. He has his own name for his crew, but I call mine my Executive Board.

Any successful corporation has an executive board of individuals who presumably guide the complex, multicelled business organism toward a bright and prosperous future. Ideally, each board member brings to the table a unique and valuable set of skills that enhances the operations of the board and, by extension, the entire company.

I figure, why not do this for a human being? Luke Skywalker

had Obi-Wan Kenobi and Yoda, plus Han Solo and Leia and Chewbacca and other teammates. Why not create a dream team of your very own?

Your executive board needn't be comprised of superstars like Baratunde or adorable animatronic puppets like Yoda. The board members should be people you trust. They should have sharp minds, good hearts, and a generosity of spirit. They may not all agree with one another, which is absolutely fine. Your aim in selecting them is to get a variety of perspectives on your life from people who are invested in your well-being but who can remain clear-eyed enough to give you a logical evaluation.

Some people have an executive board composed entirely of yes-men. I would caution against this. Don't select the friends who always think you're right. Select the friends who sometimes agree with you, sometimes disagree with you, and are willing to tell you honestly either way. Here are a few folks you might consider inviting to take a seat on your executive board.

- **The straight shooter**—He always tells it like it is, even if the truth is sometimes hard to hear. But he does it with love, always with the goal of your happiness and health. He might not talk much, but when he does, it's well worth listening.
- **The interpreter**—She might seem a little bit psychic sometimes. She's just so good at figuring out other people's motivations and needs. She'll be of special help when your mind is too clouded by anger or desire to make a clear decision. And when you just can't understand why someone

would act in a particular way, the interpreter will break it down for you.

- **The joker**—He can lighten up any situation with his wry and funny perspective. He's respectful and has a good heart, but his sense of humor may run toward the dark. That's good. You want that—somebody to leaven the tension sometimes. Also, humor can change your outlook.
- **The smartest person you know**—Who is the smartest person you know? I'm not talking book smart, although that can certainly be part of it. I'm talking about somebody who just has a wealth of knowledge on a variety of subjects. You wanna know about welding? He can tell you how to solder (and how to pronounce "solder"). Curious about the rules surrounding divorce in your state? He'll know that, too. This person absorbs information like a sponge with infinite capacity.
- **The connector**—This chick has friends in every place you've ever heard or thought of. What's more, she's willing to share contacts with you because she trusts you, she likes you, and she likes to put good folks in contact with one another. She's a valuable addition to your team, because if she doesn't know the answer to something, she knows somebody who *does*.

I think it's a very nice idea to ask somebody if they'd like a permanent position on your executive board. Make it clear that this is technically an unpaid position, but it will involve a lot of perks: free coffee or tea (you better buy it or make it, and none of that weak stuff, either); good companionship; the loan of your vehicle whenever necessary for moving large objects; and the opportunity to get your own advice on stuff any time of day or night, so long as you're not asleep or occupied with something extremely important.

You'll find that most folks are incredibly flattered to be offered such a position. Tell them they're a valuable part of your life and that, while you're not some ancient king or queen, you do see the value of having advisers on hand to help guide your world. Sometimes you may even see fit to convene your executive board in one place, in which case you should buy them really excellent pizza and maybe a case of artisanal root beer.

My instinct is that the folks on your executive board ought not to be involved with you romantically, at least not at this moment in time. At some point, you may wish to consult your executive board on things related to your romantic relationship(s).

On the same note, you may not want a close family member on your executive board. Then again, maybe your son is capable of giving you great insight, and your ex-wife has fantastic advice on how you ought to proceed in the dating zone. Go with whatever works in your world.

Don't take the formation of the executive board lightly. You don't want to have to fire one of these people one day. Look for folks who've been in your life a long time and will likely be in your life for many years to come. Don't call on them often or lightly. But when the time is right, shine your proverbial bat signal into the sky and let them know it's time to talk. They'll probably be honored to do so.

Chapter 12

TAKE CARE OF YOUR TEETH

Well, this is clearly going to be a hot and horny journey through a seductive world of intrigue. And the award for Sexiest Chapter Title of All Time goes to . . . "Take Care of Your Teeth"!

Okay, maybe not.

Good teeth are the foundation of good health. A dentist told me that once, and while he was obviously biased, I think he had an excellent point. The health of the teeth, gums, and tongue is related to virtually all other bodily systems. I could break this down for you in a more deliberate and detailed fashion, but that would take up needless time with boring science words, and I'd probably have to do a bunch of annoying research. Just trust me on this one: teeth are important.

How you do the little things in life is how you do everything in life. Dental health is an important aspect of self-care. It's not just physical; it's psychological. When we're babies, we explore everything with our mouths. The mouth is our first connection to nourishment outside the womb. It's how we experience the world before we figure out how to use our other senses. When viewed in this way, one can understand why a twice-daily (or hell, thrice-daily) dental ritual is quite a lovely way to take care of oneself. It is nurturing and kind.

Years ago, I sought out a dentist who specialized in anxious patients. As we've established, I've struggled with anxiety for most of my life. At times it has crippled me emotionally and mentally; at other times it's been a mere nuisance. Enough folks are terrified of the dentist that there are dentists out there who cleverly market themselves as anxiety-free or pain-free dentists. Many of them will drug you up to chill you out before they even take a peek inside your mouth. I was kind of hoping that would happen with this dentist. But nope. He had other plans.

This delightful Upper West Side dentist and his wife/receptionist had a good chat with me. They went over my medical history, my dental records, and my personal experience with anxiety. Then it was time for me to finally sit down in the exam room. The dentist took one look at me sitting in that chair and said, "Okay, relax your shoulders."

"My shoulders *are* relaxed," I said.

"I have a feeling you're so used to not being relaxed that you don't know what 'relaxed' is," he said. He wasn't being critical or condescending. He was being wise and observant. And he was right!

In that office, we worked with visualization techniques to deal with anxiety. We also worked with breathing techniques that I could manage even when there were various dental instruments in my mouth. I had to budget extra time for my appointments there, but then, so did he and his wife. I learned a lot from that dentist. He was a hell of a guy. And he made an ordinary ritual into something a bit more special.

What I learned from that fellow was quite simple: Don't be afraid to tell an expert when you're feeling nervous about something to do with their area of expertise! So if you're worried about a gyno exam, don't be afraid to tell the nurse and the gynecologist that you're nervous. If you get on a flight and you're scared, let the flight attendant know. Hell, tell the pilot if he's hanging around. Most of the time, these people are more than happy to help you feel more at ease. Now, whenever I go to a dentist, I tell him or her that I'm a bit nervous. And guess what? They're used to it.

After my insurance changed, I started seeing a dentist in a fancy office building closer to Midtown. This guy was great. He was a real charmer, handsome and funny and delightful. I knew right away that I could chat with him and be honest about my fears. I also mentioned I carried anti-anxiety medication with me just in case of panic attacks.

"That's fine!" he said. "We're going to do our best to make it as painless as possible. You do your breathing. If you need to take a pill, just let us know and we'll get you water."

This proved to be useful down the line, particularly when I needed a root canal (oh joy of joys). Eventually, I came to enjoy these visits (except for the occasional pain, of course). Everyone in that office was interesting, great at telling stories, and fond of excellent pop music from the 1980s. Why wouldn't I want to hang out with these people?

I referred a girlfriend to his practice because she hadn't seen a dentist in fifteen years and I knew he'd be great with her. I was right. He was slow and careful and methodical. His receptionist was warm and his dental hygienists were kind. My friend had to make four visits to the dentist just for a regular cleaning—there was so much plaque buildup in her mouth that they attacked it in quadrants. She was scared each time, and each time somebody held her hand and told her she was going to do great. Of course, by the fourth time, she was far less scared, and they were all friends. And you know what else? She had no cavities. None. I get a cavity if I look at a cupcake. That gal didn't go to the dentist for fifteen fucking years and she was fine. Sigh. (But seriously, fuck her.)

This dentist made a point of telling my friend that while going to the dentist can be unpleasant, it's important. And she wasn't a flosser (still, no cavities!), so he taught her how to floss properly.

"It's a good, easy way to take care of yourself," he said. "Just a few minutes a day. Brush your teeth in the morning, do it midday if you like, and floss and brush at night. Be gentle—you don't have to rub your gums raw. Treat yourself nicely." Now she actually looks forward to going to that office a couple of times a year, because she's one of their great success stories and they all fawn over her. Still no cavities. What a monster.

Many years ago, I volunteered in a dental clinic in the South as a translator for migrant workers. My Spanish was decent then, and I actually enjoyed learning the different technical terms. Most free clinics for the very poor do two things: cleanings and extractions. Some only do checkups and extractions. I saw very clearly how closely dental health is linked to the rest of the body. I also saw how dental health is linked to economic privilege. The dentist and I talked about it once.

"The best thing we can do here," he said, "is teach people

how to do as much of their own dental care as possible. In the long run, it will save them enormous amounts of time and money."

On all levels, taking care of one's teeth is important. There is the physical aspect. There is the financial aspect. There is even the emotional aspect—it's a good way to show yourself you care, that you know you've got inherent worth and that you deserve to be treated nicely. So even if you're afraid of the dentist—or you cannot afford to go to the fancy dentist who specializes in talking about feelings—you can get your hands on some toothpaste, a toothbrush, and some floss. It's a small thing to do, but it's a very nice thing to do. Your body will thank you for it, and so will your mind and your wallet.

Chapter 13

STOP APOLOGIZING FOR EVERYTHING

I'm sorry. I'm so sorry. I'm really, really sorry. I'm sorry I looked at you while you were watching TV. I'm sorry I lowered the window. I'm sorry it's not organic. I'm sorry I got you so many Christmas presents. I'm sorry I cut my hair without asking you first. I'm sorry I applied to school. I'm sorry I wrote a book and didn't ask for your input. I'm sorry I said yes to that gig. I'm sorry I didn't get a higher grade. I'm sorry I gained all this weight. I'm sorry I lost all that weight. I'm sorry I sent two texts in a row, and I know this is the third one but I just want to say I'm sorry. I'm sorry I don't do coke. I'm sorry I got drunk. I'm sorry my vagina is so sensitive.

I'm sorry my vagina is so sensitive.

There's a moment at which every junkie hits rock bottom. I think that was mine.

I'm an apology addict. Most women I know are similarly afflicted. We think our value as females is dependent on being literally and figuratively pliable to the point of contortions that would make a pretzel jealous. And in so doing, we not only devalue our actual important and genuine apologies but posit ourselves as being ever in error, constantly overspeaking, overspending, overlaughing, overcrying, overeating, overexisting.

Men fear not being enough. Women fear being too much.

I'm sorry my vagina is so sensitive.

This is a thing I actually said to a man who wielded his erect penis with all the delicacy of a public works employee jackhammering through concrete. There's making love, and then there's some good old-fashioned *fuckin'*. I'm pretty sure he thought he was doing the latter, but it actually felt as though he were attempting to shove my cervix up into my throat. To be fair to him, he was genetically blessed with an overabundance of drilling equipment. To be fair to me, my vagina is not constructed of reinforced steel.

I'm sorry my vagina is so sensitive.

I'm sorry my favorite and most treasured mucous membrane, the most sensitive part of my body, which happens to be attached to a wee nubbin that contains more concentrated nerve endings than any other organ in the human body, male or female—I'm sorry it feels so many things. *Lo siento. Mi dispiace. Je suis désolée.*

The worst part is that he was a good dude and probably would've responded kindly if I'd only had the guts to ask him to go slower. Instead, I apologized for not having a vagina that was impervious to pain, and then I irrationally resented him for it.

I have apologized to tables for strolling into them. I have apologized to doors for walking into them. I have apologized to clothes for accidentally ripping them.

It may seem like there's a long leap from apologizing for bumping into an inanimate object and, say, apologizing for a traumatic flashback, but I don't think so. Words have the power to form our experience and thus our reality. The more unnecessary apologies we make, the more we unwittingly convince ourselves that we are at fault for everything—even a vicious crime in which we were the terrified victim.

We are a generation that arrived pre-empowered thanks to the work of our moms and grandmothers and great-grandmothers. We're smart, we're ambitious, we're hardworking, we're determined, we're badass, we're brilliant—and we're still so very, very sorry.

I wonder when we'll stop apologizing for existing.

Chapter 14

RADICAL OVERCONFIDENCE

The young Canadian writer Sarah Hagi once said, "Lord, give me the confidence of a mediocre white man." It's one of the smartest things I've ever heard (besides the tweet where Sarah claimed the reason she wears a hijab is because she keeps a tiny Voldemort in there, but that's another hilarious tale). Because as we see frequently, mediocre white men rise to positions of great power and prestige in part by virtue of the belief that they deserve said rewards. Put another way: A reasonably qualified straight white man walks into a job interview, and we can assume the gig is his until he proves otherwise. Anybody else walks into a job interview—even with glowing credentials—and we can assume the gig *isn't* hers until she proves otherwise.

I'm aware that I'm making sweeping generalizations here. And by the way, if you are a white man and you are reading this book, you are clearly not mediocre. You are clearly fantastic and amazing, and you make excellent choices in reading materials and probably in life in general. You are the best that white men have to offer. Good job, and please remember to wear sunscreen.

But consider Sarah Hagi's point.

What would life be like if everybody had the inherent, unquestioned, unexamined confidence of someone from the dominant class or culture? What if everybody acted as if they had the right to walk into a store without being tailed by a security guard, or into a boardroom without being mistaken for an assistant's assistant?

What if everybody acted as if they deserved success?

So many of us are Other in some way. We are queer, or we're outside the gender binary, or we're poor, or we're disabled, or we're sick, or we're less educated than our peers. We are women and/or people of color and/or any of the other things I've just mentioned. We are bigger than what is considered fashionable. We are taller women or shorter men. We are different in some way from what is presented as normal and usual and acceptable and fine. This is not to disparage folks who do occupy that space known as "normal." It is simply to honestly acknowledge that there are people who do not live in that rarefied slice of Ken-and-Barbie real estate.

It's not entirely surprising that some of us don't have the most sparkling reservoir of self-esteem. I certainly don't have it. As I write this very essay, sitting at a hotel room desk in California, my belly hangs heavy on the thighs of my crossed legs. In fact, sometimes I'm having trouble concentrating on these words because I'm summoning images of how chunky I must look as I walk into a business meeting. In a city full of thin people with shiny white teeth and perfect hair, I feel fat and ungainly and unkempt. I don't usually let this get to me, but right now, in this moment, it's getting to me.

Right now, I picture myself walking into a big meeting this week. I've got to convince some folks that I can do an excellent job on a project. I can do the best job possible. I can really knock it out of the park. They should definitely hire me and pay me to do this gig. And as I look at myself in my mind's eye, I'm thinking, "Oh, my hair looks lousy. My belly pokes out too far. My breasts are too big in that sloppy way and they're not as high as they used to be. I look like a squat Italian housewife—not the sexy Sophia Loren kind, but the kind who chases her daughter's lover out of the house with a rolling pin. They'll laugh at me. They'll think I'm not good enough."

Now I interrupt this cycle of self-criticism and think of Sarah Hagi's words. I ask myself a few questions:

- Do my guy friends ever worry so much about their appearance before they go into a meeting? [No.]
- Do my guy friends create elaborate fantasies about how the powerful people in suits will judge them based on physical imperfections? [No.]
- Do my guy friends walk into a room with confidence? [Yes.]

What would happen if I walked into that room with confidence, too? What would happen if I acted as if I gave not one single shit about what anyone thought of my hair or my tits or my teeth or my tummy or my ass? What would happen if I went in there with the full confidence that they would be lucky to work with me? What would happen if I thought to myself, "Oh, they need me to like them," rather than "Oh, I need them to like me"?

What would happen if I engaged in radical overconfidence? I don't mean the kind of hubris that leads an ill-informed hiker to believe he can easily traverse rough terrain with insufficient water reserves and a crappy pair of shoes. I mean the kind of energy and pride and can-do attitude that refuses to be cowed by the word "no."

What would happen if I displayed chutzpah aplenty—the sass and strength that I imagine are the rightful possession of a richer, bolder, better-looking person? What would go down if I waltzed into that joint with my head high, my smile bright, my shoulders squared, and my heart brimming with the belief that I kick fucking ass?

Now that would be radical, indeed.

I know radical overconfidence works because I've used it often. I didn't come to know its power until I hit my thirties, when I realized no one was better equipped to advocate for me than, well, me. I had to be my top priority in my professional life. Rather than being sweet and unassuming, I had to be bold and brave. I could still be nice. I could still be kind. I could still celebrate other people's achievements and glean wisdom and understanding from studying their feats. I could still learn a lot from other people, and I could still be quite open about my thirst for further wisdom.

But enough of the meek shit. Enough of the trying-to-be-a-cutesy-wide-eyed-baby pantomime that women are trained to perform. If I was to get what I wanted from life—or at least from the entertainment and publishing industries—I had to act like I owned it. I had to act like I was owed it by virtue of my sheer awesomeness. I had to display radical overconfidence.

You know that saying, "Fake it till you make it"? That's part of radical overconfidence. If somebody asks you, "Do you have experience managing a coffee shop?" and you only filled in once or twice for your manager at Starbucks five years ago, say, "Yes.

Yes I do." Then study up on the rules and procedures in your new workplace. Show up early to prepare. Throw yourself into the work. Learn from others. Keep your mind open. Breathe to center yourself. Don't lose your cool. You know you can do this. You know you can get through the day and come out a winner. Mistakes will be made. That's natural. But you're a hard worker and a smart person. You've got this. You can do this. And every day, you're going to be a bit better than the day before.

Now, I don't suggest employing my strategy if, say, you're a surgical resident and somebody says, "Hey, have you ever done brain surgery all by yourself?" Um, when we're talking life-or-death situations, let's stick to what we know. But when we're talking a chance to make some sweet, sweet cash doing something difficult but ultimately not life-threatening, you've got some room to feign a kind of confidence you may not yet have. I'm not advocating you outright lie. I'm advocating you sell your own talents with as much zazz and panache as a car dealership might use to advertise a vehicle.

Radical overconfidence doesn't mean you look down on other people or you disrespect the need to work hard. In developing a pitch for a film version of a novel I wrote, I mentioned to a friend that the business folks wanted a pretty detailed presentation.

"Ugh," he said, rolling his eyes. "That's so annoying. They should just trust that you've got it. I mean, you wrote the book."

"Yes," I said. "I did write the book. But a film is different than a book. And I understand that I've got to show that I know how to tell a story on-screen, not just on the page."

"Don't let them psych you out," he said.

"That's not what I'm doing," I said. "I'm going to go in that room and own it. It doesn't matter that I've never adapted one of my books to a film before. I've done it for television, and that's a great start. Everyone gets a first shot, and I've earned this one. I know I can do it because I've done the work to prepare and I'm more than willing to do the work to see this thing through."

"I hope you get it," he said. "I know you can do it."

"I hope I get it, too," I said. "It would be a smart investment on their part."

That's radical overconfidence. I didn't say, "I am the greatest writer of all time and anyone who doesn't recognize this is a fool!" I merely acknowledged the reality of the situation: it would take hard work, and I was willing to put the hard work in. And I recognized that, having created the characters and the story for a novel, I was uniquely suited to tell the story in a new format.

Radical overconfidence is walking into a performance evaluation and singing your own praises while tactfully acknowledging areas in which you're working to grow. Radical overconfidence is telling your boss that your work has merited a raise—and then backing up your assertion with facts, figures, and hard evidence of your own awesomeness. Radical overconfidence is wearing a sleeveless dress when the magazines say your upper arms are too big for sleeveless dresses. Radical overconfidence is telling a lover how to give you an orgasm rather than being quiet and hoping it just happens, like some kind of sex magic.

I know you can do it. And on some level, you know you can do it. So identify an area of your life in which some radical overconfidence would help you kick ass. And then go out and kick said ass! Life is too short to waste time pretending to be small and inconsequential when you are actually as vast and powerful as a distant star.

Chapter 15

JOIN THE **FANCY CLUB** AT THE AIRPORT

Sometimes, because we were born into a certain class or treated a certain way, we don't think we deserve the nice things. We can't imagine rewarding ourselves with fancy stuff, because nobody ever told us we could or should. Plus, we were raised to be thrifty and sensible and we shouldn't spoil ourselves, right? What if we got too used to the finer things in life? Then we'd turn into assholes, probably. Right? Right?

Bullshit.

You deserve all the awesome, upscale crap in the world. I know you can't access all of it—neither can I. But you can probably access some of it. You just don't know you can because *they* don't want you to know you can. Who is *they*? The Establishment, obviously. It's probably a conspiracy to prevent the masses from rising up and claiming what's theirs, but that's a whole other book and I think Karl Marx already wrote it.

I used to breeze past the fancy club at the airport. You know the one I mean—the one hidden away from the rest of the mass and rabble. It's in your terminal, and you wonder what it's like in there, but you figure it's only for rich people, and anyway you're in a rush to get to your gate.

Then I had a particular trip from LAX back to New York. Apparently, weather disasters had struck in like eighteen different parts of the country. Every outlet in the regular airport was taken. Every seat was gone. I couldn't even get into one of the restaurants, like McDonald's (mmmm) or Googly O'Houlihan's or whatever. You know what I'm talking about—those fake airport restaurants that try to seem like regular restaurants but are actually just way stations for the bedraggled and the pissed off. They're depressing, and they offer you plastic cutlery, but damn, are they a lovely place to rest your weary tuchus. And they usually give you unlimited refills on iced tea!

I wandered aimlessly for an hour or so, amid the shouting crowds, fighting back my agoraphobia and panic. Random people broke out into screaming fits. Women and children were crying. It became apparent I wasn't getting out of LAX anytime that afternoon. Or that night, probably. But I couldn't leave, because I didn't have enough time or money to grab an overnight hotel room (and they sure as shit weren't offering up free hotel rooms). What was a gal to do?

Then an angel appeared in the form of a wandering human in an airline uniform. She had been deployed to soothe the enraged hordes, and was meeting with very little success.

"Hi," I said. "I know you're really busy, and I bet people are being really nasty to you."

"It's my job," she said, grinning. "It's . . . interesting."

"Is there some secret place I can go to hang out?" I asked her. I was half joking.

"Well," she said, "you can go to the airport chapel. It's

nondenominational, but they do hold services there a few times a day. Nobody will kick you out, and you can just relax for a while. It's in the other terminal, though, and you should probably hang around here just in case they decide to give your flight the go-ahead."

"Ooh, good call," I said, filing away the chapel idea for future use. (It's great! Find one wherever you go, regardless of your discomfort with religion! It's quiet and nobody ever uses it! You can always just hide in the bathroom during Mass or whatever.)

She thought a moment and lowered her voice conspiratorially.

"You know," she said, "we do have a lounge."

"Yeah," I said, "but I'm not a member."

"First class gets in for free," she said.

"Oh, I'm in coach," I said.

Then she lowered her voice to an actual whisper.

"You can buy a day pass," she said very, very softly.

"No fucking way!" I said loudly, then clapped my hand over my mouth.

"Is it like a hundred dollars?" I whispered.

"Nope," she said, and winked. "Forty bucks. And between you and me—you got another few hours to go, most likely. I can't be sure yet, but it's one of those days."

"Got it," I said, and nodded at her like we were in a secret club and had just buried a body together.

I figured I'd spend at least fifteen dollars at one of those airport restaurants, if I could get a seat, but they would likely only let me hang out for an hour or two. Maybe this forty-dollar thing was actually a good deal.

After turning it over in my head, I was still a little suspicious. So I went up to the lounge entry and chatted the receptionist up.

"What's it like in there?" I asked.

And then she told me.

Access to the lounge meant free Wi-Fi, a free soft chair in which to nap, a free bathroom *with showers* (I didn't use one, of course, but they were very clean! I checked!), and all the free snacks I wanted! Like, *good* snacks, too. Clif Bars and hearty stuff like that. Fresh fruit. Off-brand Chex Mix that tasted almost as good as the real thing. And ginger ale on tap! Ginger ale is the most soothing thing in the world to me, besides mint tea or a carefully timed masturbation session. I love ginger ale! Plus I could have coffee and tea and a bunch of free newspapers. Lots of television sets. So many electrical outlets so I could plug in and watch whatever I wanted on my laptop. They had meals you could order, but I didn't need any of that because there was so much free shit. Also, everyone who walked out the door looked more peaceful and serene than anyone I'd seen out in the regular part of the airport.

I forked over the forty bucks and sailed on into the promised land. And you know how long I was in there? Twelve hours. *Twelve. Hours.* That $40 ended up factoring out to about $3.33 an hour. You think it was worth it? You're gosh-darned right it was worth it! I made new friends from all over the world. I am not in contact with any of them today, but they had very interesting romantic lives and work complaints and photographs of their grandchildren. I slept for at least two hours. I got a bunch of work done. I watched some very dramatic television news programs. I got to know all the lounge workers.

Now, as those twelve hours went on, more and more people

came into the lounge. Word had spread of the mighty day-pass experience. But the lounge could hold only so many people, and they put a cap on it after a few hours. So the lounge got crowded, but never so crowded that I couldn't find a seat. Eventually I just started looking at the other people as friends I hadn't met yet. Some of them responded in kind. (A few wanted nothing to do with my friendly greetings, which I totally understood—I had been up for a long time and may have ceased making logical sense at a certain point in my stay.)

Pretty soon, I was basically the self-appointed host of that joint. If you looked confused trying to find the bathroom, I'd pop up and help you out. If you seemed befuddled by the array of snacks on offer, I was happy to advise you on the best pairing with the *free wine they started giving out*. It was my party, and everybody was invited (so long as they had a pass).

It got to where you could distinguish the day passers from the members. The members were generally clad in nice suits or at least decent sweatpants. They walked around with casual ease and took the free things without question. The rest of us were amazed by it all.

"Can I really have these Oreos for free?" one of us would ask in wonder.

"Why, yes," the attendant would say graciously. "Enjoy."

By the time my flight actually boarded, I was in a great mood. And I was sorry to leave all my new friends at the fancy airport lounge. I really got to a place where I felt like I could survive there forever. Even the toilet paper was nicer than the kind they had out in the public restrooms.

Softened and soothed by my half day of pure luxury, I glided into the airplane with a benevolent smile and a contented sigh.

Then I sat next to an evil screaming child for six hours. He used his game device with no headphones on, because his mother sucked and he sucked.

But you know what? I dealt with it. I was okay. Because I had my own headphones, and they (mostly) drowned him out. Also, I'd just spent twelve hours bathed in serenity. It honestly motivated me to work harder and look for more opportunities, if only so I could have the pleasure of using those airport lounges whenever I pleased.

Today, I'm more able to afford those day passes (though that membership remains out of my league). Still, I don't always visit the lap of luxury. Sometimes they're out of the way and inconvenient. Sometimes they cost a lot more than forty dollars for a day pass. And sometimes they really are members only. But I still do it once in a while, just to remind myself that I can and that I deserve a break, just like any of the fancy people. And so, dear reader, do you.

Chapter 16

WHEN **YOU CAN'T** FIGURE SOMETHING **OUT**, PUT **YOURSELF** IN WATER

Because we are human and not divine, we will inevitably run into issues that are beyond us. We think and we think and we think some more, until our heads actually hurt. We ask everybody else for the answer, and no one can give it to us. We buy excellent books chock-full of fabulous advice about all sorts of things (ahem), and yet we *still* can't figure it all out. What gives? What's the deal? Why is life so confusing?

As befits its fluid nature, water is changeable and mutable and dynamic. So are we. Sometimes getting in the water can remind us of this. Sometimes getting in the water is like having a little moment back in the womb.

Get into the nearest bathtub, river, lake, or ocean. Even a swimming pool can work, if you've got one handy. And if none of that seems possible, stand in the shower for a few minutes and feel the droplets pelt your skin.

On a recent bidness trip, I found a discount rate at a hotel across the street from the ocean. As soon as the taxi turned the corner and the ocean came into view, I felt better. And when I smelled the salt air and listened to the waves crash, some of the tension went out of my body. I felt how small I was in comparison to the vast ocean, and I felt grateful.

You may not have an ocean right by your house, and even if you do, the weather may not be fabulous. That's okay. Throw a handful of sea salt in a warm bath. Light a candle, get in there, and soak. You may just find that something will shift. And if not, at least you'll be cleaner and less stinky. I consider that a spiritual win, too.

Oh, and if you can't put yourself in water, I suggest putting water in yourself. I recently started a health plan that requires me to drink so much water all the time. Sometimes I have it in the form of tea or coffee (no milk or sugar added, except when I'm feeling extremely wild), but generally I drink my water straight with no mixers. I am amazed at how much more alert I feel. I'm also constantly in the bathroom, because my bladder is the size of a very, very tiny walnut, but I'm told this is a healthy, natural, good thing. Drinking lots of water clears my mind, my spirit, and my digestive tract. I could pay a stranger a hundred dollars to shove a tube up my asshole for the very elaborate pseudoscientific shit-milking that is "colonic irrigation," but I prefer to take my water the way Baby Jesus intended: through the mouth and down the hatch. I suggest you do the same—for me, but also for Baby Jesus.

Chapter 17

TAKE THE COMPLIMENT

The women's restroom at a big party is an emotional mine-field.

"Hi! You look great in that dress!"

"Oh my God, my arms look *so fat,* but thank you."

"Your hair looks amazing."

"Ugh, have you *seen* my roots? They're legit gross."

"Hey, congratulations on getting married today at this fine and extravagant wedding we're at."

"Oh, yeah, I mean, it'll probably end in divorce because I'm so unlovable, but thanks."

Okay, maybe that last exchange was a bit of an exaggeration.

Maybe.

Women are trained to never, ever, ever, ever take a compliment. We must deflect kind words at every turn, replacing them with self-mockery, self-deprecation, self-sabotage. There's a wonderfully telling sequence in the film *Mean Girls* when the American-raised girls take time to stand in front of the mirror and tear their appearances apart. Lindsay Lohan's character, who was raised mostly around her parents and one little-boy friend in a remote area somewhere in Africa, has no experience with this time-honored ritual. She doesn't understand that she's supposed to participate in order to fit in. It makes no logical sense to her, because it would make no logical sense to any reasonable human being.

It's a real challenge to take a compliment. It's hard to accept praise when you're constantly made aware of your own inadequacies, of the ways in which you fall short of the Great American Ideal (or Great Canadian Ideal, or Great Wherever You're Reading This Book Ideal—I'm particularly psyched if you're reading it in another language, because that means my agent sold foreign language rights and we earned a check, hooray!).

I focus on women here because I'm a woman, but I know men who have a really difficult time with praise—particularly if they had highly critical parental figures. They simply do not know how to take a compliment. It makes them incredibly uncomfortable. They don't like the spotlight of personal adulation shone on them. They prefer to be known for the things they do rather than the person they are. They might be able to deal with, "Hey, man, nice PowerPoint presentation!" because they can distance themselves from the praise. It's not really for them; it's for a thing they made. These guys certainly would hate to hear "I love you, man!" or "You're a hell of a great guy" or "You're supercute." Awkward! Embarrassing! AAAK!

This past winter, I was at a small dinner party at the home of my friend Catherine and her husband, Joshua, and their wee handsome imp of a son. Catherine is the artistic director of the

Moth, a fabulous nonprofit live-storytelling extravaganza that has spawned various books, workshops for city kids, a very successful podcast and public radio show, and plenty of great performing careers. She's got lots of interesting friends and associates, and on this particular frigid New York evening I met a gal who was very clearly a badass artist of some kind. She was very beautiful and striking and I immediately wanted to impress her. She had lived in New York for years and seen the comprehensive transformation of much of the city over successive mayoral administrations. She had great stories. I liked her right away.

We got to chatting, and I mentioned that I was rather uncomfortable with my brand-new hair color (it was an ill-advised attempt at blond, a journey many women take with varying degrees of success at some point in their lives). We talked about hair, and then got onto other subjects. After about forty-five minutes, the woman said, "You know, since we started talking, you've apologized for your hair twice. And you've apologized for not wearing any makeup. Why do you think I would need you to have a different hair color or lots of makeup? Do you think those things would make me like you better?"

Well, she just about blew my mind with that one. First of all, I hadn't realized I'd apologized for my hair. I knew I'd mentioned it, but the apology had been so automatic that I hadn't even processed it as such. And I'd done it twice. Then I'd apologized for not wearing any makeup, as if my appearance sans mascara would offend this potential new friend.

"Wow," I said. "You're right. I'm sorry." And then, after a pause, we both started laughing.

"I think your hair looks great," she said.

"Oh, well . . ." I searched for the right response. "Thank you?" I said.

"There you go," she said.

It is so ingrained in us to reject praise and compliments. Sometimes this is because we genuinely do not believe we are worthy of them. Sometimes this is because we feel the proper thing is to appear humble, even if we, in fact, are not.

There's a phenomenon in Australia, New Zealand, and other countries called "tall poppy syndrome." It's the idea that someone who has achieved much must be regularly cut down to size in order to fit in with the rest of the community. It seems to occur when people grow envious of a person's success. I think we have a version of this in the United States, although here we are vastly more open to braggadocio and bravado. But there is still the notion that one who works very hard and displays great talent ought to be quite humble and unassuming about it, as if it just sort of happened by the grace of Fate or happenstance.

Fuck. That.

Look, I'm all for a person displaying gratitude to the greater forces at work in her life. If you feel God has helped you succeed, by all means, give it up to God! And I'm not saying one needs to declare oneself the greatest ________ in the world every time one leaves the house. But at the very least, when you're given praise that another person feels you've rightly earned, you can take the compliment. It's like accepting a gift from someone, a gift they really want to give you.

Think about it. If you see a friend who looks particularly stunning at work one day and you say, "You look amazing today, Sheila!" do you *really* want Sheila to blush and say, "Oh, God, I look like a living nightmare"? No, of course not! You want Sheila to say, "Thank you. That is so nice of you." Wouldn't that be great? It would also be rather efficient, as it would save you the energy of wasting time going, "No, Sheila, I mean it, you look fantastic!" while Sheila goes, "Oh, but look at this run in my stocking" and so forth.

You can take the compliment and give one in return, if that makes you feel better. But guess what? You can also *just take the compliment*. Isn't that bananas? It's true, though! You can just say, "Oh, thank you very much," and smile benevolently, not unlike a queen. You aren't obligated to make up something in return. In fact, it may sound more sincere if you don't return the compliment in that moment, but instead save something for later, when you *really* mean it. That way, the other party knows you aren't simply bullshitting her out of social obligation.

Most of us aren't showered with compliments every minute of every day. Most of us get compliments here or there, once in a while. And even then, even when they're precious and hard to come by, we're inclined to automatically reject compliments. Perhaps it's because we're so used to *not* getting compliments and *not* getting praise that it feels really uncomfortable and even frightening to deviate from the norm. Quite often, we humans prefer what is familiar to what is healthy. And if what is familiar is a sense of mediocrity or failure rather than the thrill of success, well, we're probably going to stick with what we know best.

I've heard some parents warn against giving kids too many compliments lest they grow up in a world in which they feel entitled to unearned praise. I'd say that's a fair concern, but we've got to show our kids love and appreciation, too. When I talk to kids, I try to praise them on something they've done and make the connection between their effort and the result. For example, my best friend Katy's daughter, Cora, is quite young but quite verbal. So I might say to Cora, "Cora, you just used a really big word. That was a very impressive and smart thing to do. Where did you learn that word?" On some level, I feel that's more useful than saying, "Oh, Cora, you're so smart!" Similarly, I think I'd rather tell Cora that I love the very beautiful and creative way in which she chose to fix her hair rather than just saying, "Oh, Cora, you are so pretty! Aren't you a pretty girl? Who is the prettiest girl?" Of course, I'm also going to mention to Cora that she is extremely beautiful and inherently a fucking genius, but I'm going to mix it in with compliments that acknowledge her agency and her own active participation in being a rock star kid.

When I was a kid, from when I was about nine years old, I was always told that I had a great body. From when I was very small and first sprouted boobs, I was informed that I had a really smokin' bod (although not in that exact language, thank God). And as I grew up, I was naturally fairly slender, with huge tits. I took it for granted that my body would always be this way. I remember being about thirteen and thinking, "Well, my face isn't pretty, but I've got this body adults keep commenting on. Maybe that'll just be my thing."

"You're so lucky you're naturally thin," the women in my family would say. And then they'd go on to talk about whatever diet they were on, and whatever goal weight they were trying to achieve.

Then when I was in my twenties, my body started to change. I'd never had a flat tummy, and suddenly I had fat rolls in places I'd never noticed fat rolls before. I gained ten pounds in less than a year, and a boyfriend said, "I'm just worried if you continue to gain weight, I won't find you visually attractive anymore." I found this deeply insulting, but I also found it to be completely reasonable. I resolved that I would lose weight somehow. But because I'd always been "naturally" thin, I had no idea how to go about doing it. This thing that had always been my badge of honor was suddenly going away, and I had no idea how to get it back. I'd never earned it in the first place, and had wrongly assumed this was just the way my life was always going to be. I felt helpless and ashamed.

The trend continued as I entered my thirties, particularly after I began taking a medication that has weight gain as a side effect. I got bigger and bigger and felt worse and worse about myself. When people told me I looked pretty or I looked sexy or I looked good, I thought they felt sorry for me. I'd often counter their compliments with, "Yeah, maybe when I lose fifty pounds" or, "Well, I was prettier when I was thin." Sometimes I would say this out loud, and sometimes I would say it inside my head.

Eventually—thanks in part to my interaction with that cool chick at the dinner party—I realized, *Oh my goodness. When I reject people's compliments, I'm rejecting their honest opinion and I'm also rejecting my own worth. Over and over again, I'm saying, "Hi, Nice Person—you're wrong about me. Also, I don't deserve to feel good about myself." How is that any way to live?*

So you're imperfect. So you weigh more than you'd like to, or less (having gone through a disordered eating phase at one point when I was young, I can tell you that yes, some people do in fact wish they weighed more!). So your hair isn't the exact color you wish it were. So you look back on that presentation you made at work last week and wish you had thought to include this part or to remove that part. So you're not the best parent in the world all the time.

When somebody notices something beautiful and wonderful and good about you and cares enough to tell you so, *take the compliment*. Really. I'm serious. Take it. Accept it as a gift. You're going to have plenty of experiences like the ones I described above, when you feel as if your body has betrayed you, when you feel as if you're not good enough or attractive enough or *enough* enough. Compliments are lovely little presents from human beings who may not even realize what a service they're doing you. A sincere compliment is a blessing indeed, and it's one you deserve, whether you feel you've earned it or not.

Take the compliment. And just for a moment, allow yourself to entertain the idea that you may be far more spectacular than you realize. I promise, you are infinitely better than you've ever imagined.

Chapter 18

GO **FUCK** YOURSELF (NO, **REALLY!** **MASTURBATION IS** IMPORTANT)

Do you remember those vibrating squiggle pens from the nineties? They were battery-operated, and they dispensed ink on one end by virtue of a little whirring engine on the other end. Said engine was safely encased in plastic, perhaps in the shape of a bunny or a bear. I'm pretty sure a squiggle pen was my first vibrator. I was probably eight or nine.

Masturbation is a great and glorious thing. Everyone should do it! And while I doubt anyone who picks up this book is a masturbation virgin, it is possible. And to those people, I say: The time is now. Put down the book, and get to it.

Well, first finish reading the book. Then get to it.

Women have an amazing array of options from which to choose, whether you're into dildos or vibrators or vibrating dildos or those little bullet-shaped personal massagers or the Hitachi Magic Wand or anything else. And guys can use their hands, or a Fleshlight, or (so I've heard) a warmed-up melon with a hole cut in the side. (I have no specific details on how this is achieved, sorry. Please don't burn your dick.)

Many of us were taught that masturbation is evil, a sin in the eyes of God. This is obviously false. Because even if God is real, God would never be anti-masturbation. Masturbation is awesome, and plenty of wild animals practice it, and it promotes love and peace and joy and personal satisfaction. So why did some so-called Holy Scriptures lie to us and tell us masturbation is a sin? I'm not sure, but I'd wager it has something to do with the power of shame. If you can convince someone to be ashamed of her own body, you can convince her of anything. So if you tell her a Big Giant Thing in the Sky doesn't want her to have orgasms unless she's trying to conceive a child, well, she's probably going to believe it. And then put money in the collection plate and pray for forgiveness. Convenient how that works.

Anyway, if you're looking for great resources on masturbation, I advise you to check out the online and in-store offerings provided by Babeland, a wonderful chain of sex-toy shops. You can call them up and ask a sales associate a question, or you can search their website. You'll learn so much! Don't be shy; they've heard it all.

Masturbation is an affirmation of independence and freedom. It's a wonderful way to take care of yourself, by yourself. It's as American as apple pie, or fucking an apple pie. It's your patriotic duty, and I urge you to get to it.

Chapter 19

WEAR A WEIRD HAT

Some of my favorite people in history have worn weird hats. For example: Abraham Lincoln, Albus Dumbledore, any decent French mime, Kelly Clarkson circa 2004, Indiana Jones, and other great and powerful humans. If I'm ever at a party or a parade or a sewing circle and I don't know whom to befriend, I am likely to go for the person in the weird hat. Not the potential date rapist's standard-issue bro fedora, or "brodora," mind you—that hat is not weird; it is a red flag. But weird hats are awesome.

I once wore a fabulous weird hat to a wedding. It was more of a fascinator, but we're going to call that a hat. It was white and lavender and feathered and perfect, and I paired it with major cleavage. It wasn't the classiest ensemble ever, but I looked hot and got ogled by a bunch of attractive people of all genders, so I consider it a win. I know the boobs helped, but I like to think the hat is what truly signaled, "I'm fun! I'm flirty! I'm ready to party!" Continuing its presence at elaborate high-class rituals,

I later wore it to cohost an adult film industry awards ceremony with the graceful, charming, and multitalented Stoya.

People who wear hats are people with a statement to make. They want attention. The exception is the celebrity in the baseball cap and sunglasses, who does not want attention. Leave this standoffish famous person alone. But I encourage you to seek out the grandma in the Sunday church hat, who deserves all the compliments in the world. Respectfully acknowledge the grandpa wearing the fez, the little kid wearing the Minnie Mouse ears, and the pretentious high school student wearing the beret and smoking furtively outside art class.

I wish presidents still wore hats to address the press and public. Can you imagine how cool it would be to see Obama in a hat? At least 10 percent of Bush II's war crimes might have been forgiven if he'd worn an adorable newsboy cap to White House press conferences. Bill Clinton was born to wear a backward baseball cap and I'm only sorry I've never seen him in one. Bush the Elder would've looked cute in some kind of Charlie Chaplin bowler situation. And Reagan should have taken the oath of office in his cowboy hat.

Like masks, hats can lend mystery or reveal personality. The next time you're feeling frumpy or less than fabulous, put on a weird hat. Yes, this goes for you, too, gentlemen. Put on a stovepipe hat. Put on a straw boater. Put on one of those nineties raver hats that look like Cat in the Hat or whatever. Sure, you might look like a bizarre individual, but who cares? Your spirits will rise, and you'll get a little spring in your step. You'll get some grins out of strangers, and little kids will gaze at you in wonder. Is there any better accomplishment in this life? I think not.

Chapter 20

LISTEN

This is one of the shortest chapters in the book, and for good reason: it's about shutting the hell up and listening for once in your damn life.

If there is one thing that bugs me about some people who proclaim themselves "allies" of marginalized or oppressed groups, it is that they spend more time flapping *their* lips about *their* feelings about the movement and what it means to *them*, and less time listening to folks actually affected by the issues at hand.

By all means, express your opinion. But if you are, like me, a white, well-meaning liberal activist interested in assisting in the fight for true racial equality in the United States, it would behoove you to occasionally shut your mouth and listen when the people of color in the room talk about their personal, lived experiences with racism. No one needs to hear how racist you *aren't*, or that Italians weren't considered "white" when your great-great-grandpa came to America. Have you ever been followed around a store by a security guard when all you were looking to do was buy milk? Have you ever been pulled over and harassed because a cop says you "fit the profile" of a suspect? No? Okay, be quiet.

And when, for example, a woman of color decries white feminism, she is not necessarily speaking to you, Individual White Feminist with Hurt Feelings. Or maybe she is! Either way, why don't you sit and think before you respond? You can always push back if necessary. I know it's hard to contemplate the fact that you or I might be wrong or misinformed about something, but I promise we can still live our lives happily even if we acknowledge that, yes, we fuck up sometimes. I'm not perfect. I've done and said some regrettable, ignorant-ass shit. And I'm still learning. But guess what? We can apologize. We can learn. We can do better.

In short: There are times when your voice is vital and necessary and real. And there are times when you need to stay in your lane, and shut the fuck up.

Chapter 21

THE **POWER** OF BEING A **DORK**

One of the great shames of my life is admitting I haven't always been proud to be a dork. Oh, I've always *been* a dork—and a geek, nerd, weirdo, and freak. I was always a big reader, and I loved the King's Quest games for PC when I was a child. I'd spend hours holed up in our den, manipulating the lives of one fairy-tale character or another. I had a vivid imagination and constructed elaborate realities in my mind and on paper. I dressed my brother up in all manner of clothes and engaged him in as many creative games as he could stand. (I also once locked him in a box and turned it over and over again before releasing him from this prison. I am very sorry about that, Steve. Really.)

But after a childhood in which I was called plenty of names ("lame" and "loser" stick out, as does "Medusa," which had something to do with my cloud of curly hair and the idea that men would turn to stone if they looked at my ugly face), I decided that I would have to make some changes. One of those changes was learning how to be cool, and how to hide my dorkery from the world. After faking sick every day in order to avoid being bullied on the bus, I came to understand that while being one's true self was admirable in theory, in practice it really, really sucked.

I spent most of middle school watching the cool girls carefully. I noted where they shopped, what they wore, and how they spoke to one another, as well as to other, lesser beings like myself. It seemed clear that I would need to get acquainted with the Limited, J.Crew, and possibly American Eagle and the Gap. I would have to teach myself how to apply makeup, as my mother showed zero interest in that particular activity. I would probably need to do a sport, which was a difficult proposition because I wasn't a natural or enthusiastic athlete.

I stopped playing computer games, except when we were allowed to play Oregon Trail in the school computer lab. Everybody did that, and you could make up funny names for your characters and kill them on purpose. That was hilarious to all of us, even the popular kids. I started baton-twirling class, which does not sound cool but held a certain place of status in my hometown. You got to wear cute leotards, and run around in little soft shoes, and march in parades. It was sort of like being a gymnast and a dancer all rolled into one. I figured it would make me graceful. I figured it would make me belong.

My thick eyeglasses had to go, so in the sixth grade I obtained contact lenses. Back then, technology hadn't developed to allow folks with severe astigmatism to wear soft lenses, so I had to wear these hard little pieces of plastic in my eyes. On my first day of school with contacts, I walked into the trailer where we had social studies and heard a boy exclaim, "Who is *that*? Oh, it's Sara." Sure, he was disappointed to finally realize it was me, but for one split second, he'd thought I was hot. (A few years later, he was the first boy to ever ask me on a date. I believe my mom drove us to see the Helen Hunt–Bill Paxton tour de force *Twister*. We did not kiss.)

My eyes were frequently red, itchy, irritated, and watery as a result of the hard contacts, and in the beginning I often left class to adjust them. But I didn't care; I was so happy to be rid of my glasses. I was so excited to begin my new life as a *pretty* girl.

I figured out how to dress to fit in, but I was still fairly weird. I quit baton twirling and devoted myself full-time to social climbing. In the ninth grade, I learned how to kiss the asses of the popular kids while making them laugh. I could gain their confidence and amuse them without threatening their position of status and power. This allowed me to occupy two spaces—the nerd world, in which I felt more comfortable, and the cool world, in which I felt more alive and special.

In high school I was able to successfully navigate both worlds. My school had about two thousand students in four grades, rendering it sufficiently large to allow me to blend in when I wanted to and stand out when I wanted to. I didn't like being at home, so I packed my schedule with after-school activities, the better to keep myself occupied. In retrospect, I ought to have been playing Dungeons and Dragons and going to midnight showings of *The Rocky Horror Picture Show.* Instead, I attempted lacrosse (riding the bench for most of the season), joined and then quit the flag squad, and then settled into a life of various clubs. I put into practice the flirting techniques I'd long observed from afar. I got boyfriends. All along, college was the big prize. It was my ticket to moving out of my house and on to a fabulous new life in which I would be a crusading, Pulitzer Prize–winning investigative reporter. I tried so hard, all the time. I didn't sleep enough. My back hurt a lot. I got depressed and started taking pills. The school referred my parents to a social worker, something I thought was quite common until recently, when I realized it wasn't. That was my first experience with therapy, and thank goodness for it.

I really, really, really wanted to be perfect.

I didn't anticipate that the years of stress and strain and artifice would wear on me. It takes a lot of energy to maintain a false front. It's hard to develop different personalities to suit different people in your life. Because I lost my center, and my sense of self, I was vulnerable to the desires of other people—my parents, my teachers, my friends. Often, these people had conflicting goals. And of course, they all had their own problems, which I usually tried to fix. Fixing other people's problems gave me a sense of power and goodness and righteousness. I thought I could fix everybody and then I'd be okay, too.

After high school, I drifted apart from the popular kids. Some of them dumped me; I suppose I dumped some of them. They no longer had any use for me, nor I for them. I made the mistake of genuinely caring about one or two of them, and that was a silly thing to do. They had never loved me for me, because I had never presented my true self to them. And honestly, I didn't really know them, either. The rejection stung at first, but as I moved along and made new friends in college, it hurt less and less.

My weirdo friends stayed in touch. The ones who might plausibly have been called freaks, geeks, and burnouts were the ones who remained my real friends—in fact, some are still my buddies to this day. I learned a lot from them. They didn't disappear when I had mental health troubles. They didn't freeze me out when I dropped out of school and moved home to get my shit together. I went to their weddings and actually cared what happened (I do not, as a rule, care what happens at weddings). It meant something for me to witness their rituals of love and birth and sometimes even mourning, not because I was gaining some kind of cool points, but because that's what people who love each other do—they show up for each other as often as they can, as best they can.

And as I grew older, something even more magical began to take shape.

I began to reclaim my inner dork.

It started with the *Sandman* comics by Neil Gaiman. I don't remember who suggested I read them, but man oh man were they awesome. I got into them sometime in college, and I fell in love. They were the gateway drug to a whole host of other comics and to sequential art in general. Comic books taught me to think about the world differently. So did the *Star Wars* films—yes, even the lesser ones. I saw wonder and mystery everywhere I looked. Even *Star Trek,* something I'd previously rejected as beyond geeky, began to hold a new fascination for me.

The power of myth was so strong and so undeniable that I found myself wondering about questions of great philosophical import (*Who are we? What truly matters in this life?*) and incredibly nerdy detail. (*How does that particular imaginary weapon measure up against that other particular imaginary weapon in this imaginary world, and what would happen if imaginary weapons from other imaginary worlds traveled into this world somehow?* In other words, how would Luke Skywalker with a lightsaber fare against James Tiberius Kirk with that weird cannon he builds that fires gemstones?)

It took me years to catch on to the fact that there was a *Doctor Who* reboot. One boyfriend in North Carolina had tried to make me watch the old *Doctor Who* (can't remember which Doctor it was, but I hated the Doctor and I nearly hated the boyfriend by the end of it). This boyfriend did make excellent biscuits and was a very nice and handsome person, but I was having none of the *Doctor Who* business.

I give enormous credit to my then boyfriend for convincing me in 2010 to watch the most beautiful hour of television I've ever consumed, "Vincent and the Doctor." It is the tenth episode of series five, with Matt Smith and Karen Gillan and the delightful Bill Nighy, along with the brilliant Tony Curran as Vincent van Gogh himself. Not only did my gentleman caller ensure I'd grow to love the new show (particularly the older episodes starring my future imaginary lover, David Tennant), but he reminded me of just how incredibly gorgeous and poignant the infinitely bizarre worlds of science fiction and fantasy can be. These fanciful tales help us better understand our own world, and ourselves. (Incidentally, that particular episode was written by Richard Curtis, and that is not surprising at all when one considers that everything he writes makes me laugh until I cry, or vice versa.) I would later pay tender and sincere homage to that episode in a very ribald, raunchy novel I wrote. In art, as in life, the sublime can coexist with the earthly, and the sacred with the filthy.

What I've found in the geek world is a kind of acceptance and loving tolerance that I haven't found anywhere else. Sure, there are those folks who wish to serve as gatekeepers and arbiters of taste. There are snobs in every scene. But more often I find folks who've been bullied and abused and are simply cautious in their welcome to new friends. Once you show these folks that you're sincere and genuinely curious about their interests, they're happy to welcome you in and guide you through their fandom. You have to enter every new fandom with a sense of beginner's mind, which is to say you shouldn't show up and start waving your dick around like an expert. Respect the canon of scholarship that exists in this realm, whether it's been formally studied in the arena of academia or we're talking about various teen Tumblrs out in the world. Suspend your own sense of disbelief and ask polite questions. Understand that for some folks, the world of Pokémon is as real a world as the world of the Bible is for others. Before you giggle at that comparison—okay, go ahead and giggle, then hear me out—I would add that both worlds have been used to make shitloads of money for individuals in power, and that both worlds have been reclaimed, reinvented, and reinterpreted by people who find solace, hope, and even fun in the characters in these stories.

The symbols of geekdom have gained me friendships, connections, and entrée into various worlds. People recognize my *Doctor Who* earrings at airports, bookstore signings, parties. I know that if I wear this signifier of dorkery to a business meeting, somebody's assistant is going to get excited and point at me gleefully. I'll grin, and in that moment, I'm not nervous about pitching a project to his or her boss anymore. I've found a friend. I've found somebody I can talk a secret language with.

The other day I wandered into the office of a couple of film producers. Well, I mean, I didn't just randomly wander in—we had an appointment to have a chat. Anyway, I was a bit early, and I spied a very beautiful young woman with that kind of funky, cool lavender-silver hair that's quite hip these days. She carried herself with the grace and confidence of someone beyond her years, so I assumed she was a particularly young entertainment mogul. And I was right—this was a well-known actress and producer and singer and various other things (she's got like four million Twitter followers and people love her, but I didn't know that yet). She pointed at my earrings with that expression of glee, and I grinned at her, because I knew I had found a fellow traveler yet again. Then we freaked out and talked about *Doctor Who* for ten minutes. We concluded our meeting with a hug. Later, I learned we had a few friends in common, which surprised me not at all. Sure, we move in different worlds, but Whovians find each other. (We are called Whovians, FYI. My favorite Whovian is my friend Viviane, a Christian Republican teen. *Doctor Who* will eventually bring the world together.)

A few years back, I was on my way to the airport after a gig at the University of North Carolina at Greensboro. If I was going to make it through my morning, I was going to need some coffee. My lovely companion and I stopped in at Geeksboro Coffeehouse Cinema, and I immediately knew I was home. This place had geek décor everywhere. It had old-school video games and weird old movie posters. Best of all, it had a TARDiS, which stands for Time And Relative Dimension in Space.

A TARDiS is a time machine/spacecraft that looks like an old-fashioned British police call box but is actually just stuck looking that way. The Doctor uses it to travel around the world and the universe and through time and space. It's bigger on the inside.

Anyway, the TARDiS at Geeksboro was a big one made out of wood and it looks like the actual set piece from *Doctor Who*. Very cool stuff. I took a picture with it, met the lovely owner, Joe, and vowed that I would come do a show there one day. And then

I did! I flew down from New York City and talked about geek stuff with the nerdcore rapper Adam WarRock and the wonderful, legendary cosplay king Eddie Newsome, better known at conventions as Black Captain America (or Isaiah Bradley, an incredible Marvel character whose devastating backstory has a lot of similarities to the Tuskegee Syphilis Study). Our show was called *Growing Up Geek*, and we discussed the ways in which we were oddballs and strangers within our community, thanks to our fondness for what were considered the weirder aspects of pop culture.

Eddie's and Adam's stories are their own to tell, and they are beautiful and uplifting and truly inspiring. If you ever get a chance to talk to either of them, I suggest you reach out. They are two cool cats. Anyway, on the surface, we don't look very similar. Adam WarRock is an Asian kid raised in the American South. Eddie is a black dude raised in Newark, New Jersey. And I'm this white chick who grew up in the suburbs between Philly and New York, also in New Jersey but about a world away from Newark. Yet our tales had ample connective tissue, and we related to one another and to the audience on multiple levels. We had all been branded geeks, or dorks, or weirdos. And as adults, we had come to own our identities and love who we were and especially to love the communities that embraced us. I'm so grateful that Geeksboro co-owners, Joe and Rachel, included me in this evening of fun. (They are special adult bedtime friends—that is, they are married.)

Around the time I performed at Geeksboro, I was invited to speak at my old high school. I got onstage in the smaller of the two theaters and started talking to the kids about what it was like to be a writer and comedian. I found myself telling them plenty of funny old stories about my own adventures and misadventures at that high school. I invited them to ask questions, and they asked good ones. And at some point—I don't know how I got on the topic—I started talking about being a dork.

"I was too scared to admit that I was really a big geeky dork on the inside," I told them. "You know, I loved books and computer games and weird TV shows as a kid, but in high school I tried to repress it. I really tried to fit in and look like everybody else. I wanted to be accepted. And it worked. But I lost something in the process. It wasn't until I started owning my weirdness as an adult that I began to find success. So if you're a kid who gets bullied, if you're a freak or a weirdo or a loser, just know that you're going to do great. And if you're one of the kids who bully the freaks and the weirdos and the losers, sorry—weird kids win." I shrugged and grinned. One kid clapped excitedly. I knew he knew what I was talking about.

Then I stopped and fixed my eyes on a particular group of beautiful, shiny teens with excellent clothes and perfect hair. They were looking at me like I was an alien.

"Just wait until one of the popular kids gets into college and becomes totally bizarre," I said with evident glee. "It's gonna happen. And oh, it is glorious." Everybody laughed. I laughed, too, but I meant it.

Embrace your weird. Let your freak flag fly. Feel the power of being a dork. Maybe you won't end up on any best-dressed lists, and you probably won't be invited to the snooty parties of high society, but let's be honest: You never belonged there anyway. You belong with the rest of us in some carpeted basement somewhere, eating Cheetos and making up stories about wizards. We may not be cool, but we already love you. Join us.

Chapter 22

EVERYTHING'S NOT ALRIGHT (**AND** THAT'S **ALRIGHT**)

The worst character in the history of musical theater is Mary Magdalene in *Jesus Christ Superstar*. Andrew Lloyd Webber wastes the opportunity to create a character who is fierce, strong, and badass, and instead gives us a simpering baby woman who moons about, whining, "I Don't Know How to Love Him," because, you know, apparently a sex worker just can't possibly comprehend the notion of being friends with a dude instead of shtupping him for money. I despise her signature song for this reason and also for the simple fact that it is a terrible tune with all the appeal of long vampire fingernails scratching a dusty old chalkboard in Hell.

But Mary Magdalene is only slightly more annoying than Jesus, and the two of them are at their codependent worst in the song "Everything's Alright." Mary Magdalene is trying to keep Jesus relaxed and comfortable because his life has gotten rather stressful of late. She anoints his head with myrrh, *which is not cheap,* and Judas—who is almost always right in this play—

gets pissed off. He points out that their wacky ragtag team of desert imps could've sold that oil for several silver pieces and then donated the money to the poor. Then Jesus, in the non-comeback of the century, says that there will always be poor and he doesn't have the resources to save them all, which like, hello, if you're really God, *yes you fucking do*. And if you're not God, maybe you need to step up your human compassion game a bit, hmmm?

One of the reasons the play continues to be controversial in some quarters is that Judas functions as the voice of reason in this and other instances. And of course, Webber knows what he's doing in this scene—everything is most assuredly *not* alright, and Judas knows it, and the audience knows it, and Jesus knows it, too. It's possible that Mary Magdalene knows it as well, but it's impossible to discern her actual thoughts because she is such a bleating mess of a character. The luminous Yvonne Elliman couldn't save her in the 1973 movie, because even a gifted actress with the voice of an angel can only work with what she's given. (Yvonne Elliman later gave us the hit "If I Can't Have You," because she is good and true.)

I suppose my deep irritation with Mary Magdalene in this particular scene comes not from the quality of the writing or the music, but rather from the sentiment she expresses. Whether she believes it or not, the false proclamation that "everything's alright" seems to me to be a truly foolish way of staving off the actual danger that surrounds Jesus and Company. Wouldn't it be better to just sing, "Shit's getting crazy / Shit's getting crazy / We should all deal with thaaaaat . . ."?

I react so strongly to this because it's attached to a firm belief I maintain in my actual life, outside the theater, away from my laptop where my YouTube viewing habits lately tend toward clips from 1970s musical theater extravaganzas.

Everything is not alright. Everything is never alright. Everything is never okay. Everything is never safe. There is no place in this world, today or during the Roman occupation of Palestine or in 1973 musical theater, where one is truly inured to injury, fear, violence of the emotional or physical sort, and death.

Let's make this small and real, perhaps more relevant to our actual lives than my complaints about a Norman Jewison–directed musical film. There is endless societal pressure to pretend to be happy. This is particularly true of women, who might plausibly be expected to smile and make polite eye contact with their guards on the way to being executed by firing squad. As women, we receive the message early on that we must make things pleasant above all else, no matter the circumstances. We mustn't burden anyone else with the notion that we might be uncomfortable in the least. And if someone should ask us how we're doing, the appropriate answer is always "Good" or "Great" or, at worst, "I'm doing okay."

Everything is not alright, and that's alright. When we speak truly about how we feel, even in the context of a casual exchange at a cash register or a work function, we do others a great service—we implicitly grant them permission to be real and true and honest about how they feel, too.

Wouldn't it be great if, instead of repeating the usual mindless response to an inquiry about one's well-being, we committed to being tactfully honest? There's no need for endless details or a self-involved monologue about the nature of one's own suffering, but it seems to me to be quite appropriate to indicate when one is actually not feeling very well.

I tried this out once as an experiment at the bodega near my apartment. I was buying olive oil so that my gentleman could cook dinner, and I was loaded down with menstrual cramps and with stress over a family situation. I wasn't in the worst shape, but I wasn't in the best shape. I handed the cashier the olive oil and he rang me up.

"How you doing today?" he asked, probably out of habit because that's just what you ask strangers while you wait for their debit card to go through.

"Not great," I said, and was immediately surprised at what had come out of my mouth.

"Oh, I'm sorry," he said, with evident concern. "Are you okay?"

"I am okay," I said. "But okay is about it."

"I know what you mean," he said. "I'm having one of those days, too. It sucks." He handed me my debit card.

"Well, we're alive, right?" I said, signing the receipt.

"For now," he said, and we looked at each other and cackled darkly. I waved and left the store with my purchase.

Was it the deepest and most profound exchange two humans have ever shared? No. Did we get into the details of each other's little miseries? No. Did we waste time or embarrass ourselves or overstep each other's boundaries? No. But we were honest, or as honest as we could be in that moment, and we shared a brief bit of communion in our mutual not-alrightness. I left the store feeling at least a tiny bit more relaxed, if only because I'd gotten to vent in some small fashion.

Of course, there are times when the urge to pretend that everything is alright is superseded by enormous physical or emotional pain. In these instances, we are delivered from our usual addiction to politeness and pleasantries. I can't compare anything I've experienced to childbirth, for example, but I have gone to a place where pain was so acute that I dropped all pretense of having it together.

When I was fifteen, I found that frequent urination got in the way of my day-to-day activities. While this was most assuredly tied up in the tension and anxiety in which my home life was soaked, I didn't understand how much my life was affected by my surroundings. I certainly didn't know about the connection between stress in the family environment and physical and mental development in children and adolescents. I didn't know that sometimes folks develop responses to stress that assist them in some way—for me, escaping to the bathroom was one way to get out of uncomfortable situations. Nor had I ever heard of what is now generally called an "overactive bladder." I assume the doctors hadn't, either, since they ordered a nuclear bladder scan and cystoscopy.

A cystoscopy is a fun procedure in which a teensy-weensy camera called a cystoscope is used to examine the bladder. One may well inquire how exactly the camera gets into one's bladder. Does it magically see through skin? Does one swallow a tiny bitty camera and wait for it to somehow pass through the bladder rather than the colon? No. Instead, a tube about the size of a straw is threaded through the urethra up into the bladder. It bears a fiber-optic light source and a camera, because there's nothing more useful in diagnosing urinary problems than a good bladder selfie. A "blelfie," if you will.

The doctors also ordered a nuclear bladder scan, an even more exciting-sounding procedure in which radioactive liquids are shot into the bladder (again, through a catheter) until the patient feels full. At this point, the catheter is removed and the bladder is scanned via X-ray to see what it looks like when it's full. After that, one empties one's bladder (sometimes, as in my case, one is asked to piss the table rather than use the toilet) and doctors take more X-rays to see if one's bladder has emptied properly.

If this does not sound like a fucking tea party, that's because it isn't. For the cystoscopy, the patient can be knocked out or kept awake. They kept me awake because, they said, they needed me to be able to describe the sensations I felt—when my bladder was full, and again when it was empty.

When I lay down on the table, they covered me in a lead apron and asked if I would like for my mother to be present.

"Oh no," I said with the confident laugh of a very sophisticated high school sophomore. "I don't think she needs to see *this*."

They smiled nicely and a nurse applied numbing jelly to my urethra. Its chief characteristic was that it didn't numb anything, which I know because I could feel everything—particularly the tube with the camera as they slid it into the hole.

"Wow!" I said. "That *really* hurts." I laughed inanely, still trying very hard to act as if this were all just par for the course, no more off-putting than a casual day of shopping at Chico's or one of the other beloved stores in our suburban area.

"It'll get better as you get used to it," the doctors said. "But it will be uncomfortable."

It did not get better. It got worse. And yes, it was uncomfortable. It was beyond uncomfortable. It was really fucking painful.

That's when I began to cry.

"Do you want your mother?" they asked again.

I looked at them, my chin trembling, my nether regions exposed to the cold air of the testing room, and I considered it.

My parents are not my best friends. I respect them; I find them very interesting; I seek their opinions and I value their insight. I like to hear how they look at the world, the wisdom they've gained, the journeys they're still on. Sometimes I can't stand them. I argue with them and I make up with them. I value our time together and I value our time apart.

I have never been interested in a BFF relationship with my parents. It's not about them. It's just not my style, and it wouldn't be my style regardless of who they were.

I know girls who change in Victoria's Secret dressing rooms in front of their mothers. I know girls who sit around naked in hot tubs with their mothers, drinking beer and enjoying a fine ladies' weekend. I've just never felt the need for my mom to see me naked, nor do I feel the need to see her naked. I am aware that as she ages (she's quite young, as I was born when she was twenty-four) this will change, and that elder care often involves dropping certain dignities we've come to accept as inviolate. But I have my own friends. Not that I'm necessarily showing them my lady business, either, but anyway.

Faced with a team of doctors and nurses in masks and suits, in a cold testing room with a couple of tubes sticking out of my nether regions and images of my innards projected onto a couple of screens (one X-ray, one regular TV), I made a game-time decision to drop all pretense that everything was alright.

"If you could get my mommy," I said, my chin quivering, "that would be much appreciated."

And they got her, and she came in, all suited up in whatever Superman-proof lead suits they were all wearing, and she held my hand while I cried for the next—oh, it felt like a century, but I suppose it was no more than forty-five minutes. At home, she drew me a bath because they'd encouraged me to urinate in a warm bath, saying it would ease the pain of an inflamed urethra. It helped a tiny bit.

After a couple of weeks, the results came in. They didn't find any urinary reflux, any deficiency in the kidneys or bladder or urethra. It would seem that in that part of my body, at least, everything was, in fact, alright. And that there hadn't really been any point to those tests in the first place, probably. At least I got to watch a tiny camera plow through my urethra and bladder, live on camera. What fifteen-year-old girl wouldn't want that thrill of a lifetime?

As a bicoastal bisexual, I dwell in New York and in California when I'm not out gamboling about this fine world of ours. I love Los Angeles and New York City for different reasons, but New York City wins in at least one aspect. In New York, nobody pretends that everything is alright. If people are pissed, or uncomfortable, or scared, or even sad, you're gonna hear about it—possibly at very loud volume on the subway; possibly on the street; or possibly from within the confines of your apartment, because in my experience they've yet to invent a New York City apartment that is impenetrable to the sound of neighbors yelling at each other.

There is something enormously comforting about admitting that your life has gone mad, or that you're in a bad mood, or that you're having a tough fifteen minutes.

Try it. I wager that the sooner you drop the "everything is alright" act, the sooner everything will actually become alright, or at least manageable.

Chapter 23

LIFE IS **TOO** SHORT FOR **SHITTY** FRIENDS

Let us now discuss that most irritating of species, the most annoying creature in the colorful menagerie that is your personal life: The Shitty Friend.

I know, I know—most friends are wonderful. After all, they wouldn't be your friends otherwise, right? They're fun and silly and playful and loving, or they're serious and insightful and smart and intriguing, or they're energetic and inspiring and motivating—and if you're lucky, you get all this stuff in one person! That's how I feel about my friend Alexandra. I have a few best friends from my pre-adult years—their names are Alexandra, Katherine, Gretchen, and Rachel. They're all great in their own ways, but Alex's name comes first in the alphabet, so we're going to talk about her for the moment. Anyway, Alex is one of those all-encompassing friends who embody so many lovely characteristics at once. She always meets me where I'm at emotionally, she calls me out when I act like a jerk, though she never actually uses the word "jerk" (this has happened like twice in our friendship, but both callouts were warranted and taken to heart!), and she's generous and affectionate and kind. All in all, she's a top-shelf human, the friend equivalent of Pappy Van Winkle's Family Reserve 23-Year Bourbon. In other words, she's the good stuff.

But not every friend can be an Alex. And it's irrational to expect every single friend to live up to sky-high expectations. I don't know about you, but I'm not always the greatest friend in the world—I can be self-absorbed, narcissistic, ignorant, and plenty of other bad things. But I do think I'm generally quite a lovely friend to have, and I am fortunate to have many, many other lovely friends.

But we're not here to talk about lovely friends—we're here to talk about Shitty Friends.

Please note that we're not going to talk about actual sociopaths or murderers or anything like that. They exist and they're real and they're scary, but in this instance we're just talking about the more garden-variety version of The Shitty Friend.

There are a few subspecies of Shitty Friends I'd particularly like to highlight. Of course there are many, many other kinds of Shitty Friends in this world, not just the ones described here. Sometimes folks feel obligated to maintain false friendships with folks they've known since nursery school just because, well, they've known 'em since nursery school (or nursing school, or Camp Eagle Rock, or that summer at the beach, and so on and so forth). It's as if one must engage in a sham friendship in order to keep some vital link to the past; as if one's whole world will be turned upside down and one will lose a vast store of shared memories if one steps away from a crappy relationship with a Shitty Friend. This isn't actually true, but it *feels* true, and what *feels* true is often more important than what *is* true.

Anyway, let's explore the shittiness of a few of the most common types of Shitty Friends.

The Shitty Friend Who Never Gets in Touch: This is a very common form of Shitty Friend. We mustn't confused TSFWNGIT with The Busy Friend Who Just Had a Baby or The Slammed-at-Work Friend or The Dealing with Grief on Her Own Friend. The Shitty Friend Who Never Gets in Touch just doesn't really care about you all that much. She's never going to admit it, because that would fuck up her veneer of being a "nice" person. But she really doesn't give a shit about you. She just doesn't. Unless, of course, she wants something from you. (I would suggest being busy the next time she wants something from you.)

The Shitty Friend Who Only Loves You When You're Up: We've all been warned about fair-weather friends, right? They love you when you've got a good job, a steady cash flow, front-row seats to opening day at the local minor-league baseball stadium, one of those superfancy Sephora VIP cards, a gorgeous new car, a lake house they can chill at, a successful girlfriend who takes everybody on a fun vacation and pays for every hotel room, a rich husband who loves to throw big catered barbecues, a bit of buzz in your industry, a corner office, a superstar athlete kid, a standing reservation at the hottest restaurant in town, unlimited BOGO coupons to Lane Bryant, or whatever the hell else is cool in your neck of the woods. TSFWOLYWYU is eager to glom on to any bit of success you earn through your own hard work, and she's more than happy to take credit because you were both on the lacrosse team back in ninth grade and her influence *obviously* stayed with you all these years. She'll come sniffing around when she sees you're building a fancy new deck on your house. She'll *love* to introduce you to all her friends at the PTA meeting. She'll say things like, "OMG, girls weekend!" as soon as you mention you got a promotion at work. You'll notice this friend disappears as soon as you ask for help that wouldn't provide her with an immediate reward in the form of brownie points or actual cash money. TSFWOLYWYU is usually very obvious, although not always as transparent as one would think. However, once you identify a friend as TSFWOLYWYU, it's fairly easy to get rid of her.

The Shitty Friend Who Only Loves You When You're Down: Now *this* is a particularly insidious brand of friend. Until very recently, I didn't even know this type of friend existed! I thought everyone wanted to take the ride up the glorious mountain of success with you. I thought abandonment only happened when you were down and out, like in rock-and-roll movies where the band falls off the *Billboard* charts and everyone abandons them until they write their big comeback hit. But I was recently talking to smart human writers Chuck Wendig, John Scalzi, and Gwenda Bond via Twitter, and we all found that we had experience with this sort of friend. I thought it might be because we're all artists, a notoriously persnickety lot, but many folks from various fields also chimed in on our discussion. Anyway, TSFWOLYWYD is always there for you when you're in trouble. She's the first to offer up her couch when your wife kicks you out. She'll lend you her toolkit when you've got furniture that needs fixing. She'll listen for hours on end as you cry into the phone about your breakup. She'll give you all kinds of smart advice as you try to get yourself out of financial ruin or bring you home-cooked meals when your spouse is in the hospital. She'll bring *you* flowers when *you're* in the hospital. But where does this friend go when you get that promotion you've wanted forever? How about when your kid wins a medal in a school race? What about when you get into that MFA program or receive the grant or scholarship you've dreamed of for years? Poof! These folks disappear like cotton candy in a rainstorm (if you've been to a county fair on a stormy day, you know what I'm talking about). Sometimes they only want to deal with you when you need them, because being needed makes them feel alive. Often, they're envious of your success or good fortune; or your happiness highlights their own lack of joy. Scalzi tweeted something that I found particularly insightful: "I think that happens when people see other people's success as a referendum on their own place in life. Zero-sum thinking." Exactly.

The Shitty Friend Who Undermines You: One of the all-time shittiest friends is The Shitty Friend Who Undermines You. This person appears to stick with you through thick and thin, but needs to undermine your choices at every turn. "Oh, I *used* to like that/enjoy that/eat that/drink that/read that/think that," she'll say with passive-aggressiveness perfected over years of practice. She *won't* add, "And now I think I'm better than you because I do not do the thing that you choose to do." But she's thinking it! She's definitely thinking it. This friend undermines you because, while she may think she loves you, she also deeply resents you. You represent something she wishes she had, or something she feels she's lost. And so she must tear down your choices at every turn—but subtly and politely!

There are many more incarnations of The Shitty Friend, but those are the four with which I've had to deal the most in my own life, so I feel best equipped to describe their tendencies. And now that we have identified their chief characteristics, let's talk about how you get rid of them.

Yes, I said get rid of them. Not "have a talk" with them. Not "work through your issues" with them. Get rid of them. They are garbage people—perhaps not in their entirety, and perhaps not in the depths of their souls, where they are maybe good and pure and loving. They may be wonderful to their other friends (though I doubt it, quite frankly). They may be loving teachers, capable CEOs, great parents, remarkable athletes, empathetic nurses, insightful doctors, meticulous carpenters. But when it comes to you, they turn into trash bags full of rotting Taco Bell, and thus you must unburden yourself of their presence.

I know they've probably been hurt before, and that some of the hurt may inform their actions. But who hasn't been hurt? In the words of my friend Kimya Dawson, a wonderful artist and delightful human, "Having been fucked is no excuse for being fucked up." We've all been abused in some way. I'm not saying we've all had it equally bad or good in this life. I've marinated in privilege for years as a white woman with money and access, and thus power. I do not seek to create false equivalency between my journey and your journey and your sister's journey. But I do hold people to certain standards, and you've got to do the same, lest you be drained by vampire Nazis masquerading as, I don't know, unicorn Unitarians.

People go through rough times. They do require extra patience, love, and care. Sometimes they require forgiveness. But if you've given someone multiple chances to improve; if you've grown weary of disappointment; if you've grown fatigued by harassment, abuse, or neglect; well, my friend, it is time to do some pruning. Here are some potential paths.

The slow fade: You just stop showing up for them. You stop calling. You stop texting. You stop caring. Sure, you'll always wish 'em well, but you gotta do you. Gradually, you back your way out of their lives.

Some folks say this is a cowardly way to get out of a relationship. I disagree. At this point, you don't owe the other person anything other than basic respect. So don't, you know, leave a flaming bag of shit on your ex-BFF's doorstep. But do GTFO. And if they ask why you've been distant, you can be as honest as you like.

The fast fade: *Boom!* You're done. You cut 'em off with no explanation. This can be cruel and upsetting, or it can be equally what is necessary for you to preserve your own sanity. I can't tell you if this is the right move for you. I can't tell you if any of these methods are right for you. My job is to present them to you as options. I know this is my job because I've made it my job.

The formal breakup: This is where you sit your friend down in person or over the phone or via text or email or FaceTime or whatever and tell her exactly why you are so pissed off at her, and why you are ending your friendship. This isn't about revenge or about hurting her—and if it is, you shouldn't do it. The formal breakup is about unburdening yourself, taking a stand, getting back some of the confidence you've given away, and bringing a relationship to a definitive conclusion. I hate formal breakups and I'm terrible at them, but if you are brave enough to sit in your own power and calmly, firmly explain your boundaries, my hat is off to you.

Polite them to death: A Southern custom, this is a practice in which you become extremely passive-aggressive and evil and smile sweetly and say things like "Aw, well bless her heart" whenever the name of your "friend" comes up. You never say a bad word in public about her but you talk a ton of shit in private. As much as I adore the South and its various ways of being, I wouldn't suggest this. It'll drain you to be so sugary-sweet in public all the time, and it's fairly douchey. It's better to simply be civil when necessary and avoid spending time with the now ex-friend lest you become brittle with anger and meanness. Plus, I've done this myself, and I just ended up feeling like an asshole (because I was being an asshole).

The New Jersey: My friend once saw two drunk Jersey women fighting at a birthday party. They'd each brought the same birthday present for the family patriarch, and were enraged at each other (I think they were sisters or cousins or something). Rather than talk it out or say, "Hey, I guess he'll just return one and get something else, no big deal!" they chose to embarrass their friends and family and inconvenience everybody by being obnoxious. Now, I'm from New Jersey and I love New Jersey, but you shouldn't pull the New Jersey when you defriend someone. It's very entertaining for folks with no emotional attachment to the outcome of the fight, but it bothers everybody else. I've seen people pull the New Jersey many a time, and it often results in not speaking to each other until somebody important dies, at which point you may or may not begrudgingly say hello at the wake. (This could also be called the Sicilian.)

Before we leave this subject, I want to be clear on something: friendships are not meant to be perfect. I believe good friends help us grow and change and become better people. Sometimes that process can be painful or uncomfortable. I don't suggest dumping a lovely friend just because she's going through a rough period and can't be as present as you'd like. Nor do I suggest you expect friends to give up on you when you've hit a tough phase of your life. But there are enough people in this world who treat each other poorly, and you and your friends shouldn't engage in that kind of behavior. Ideally, a friendship should be an oasis of comfort, understanding, patience, and even frank tough love where necessary. Friends are the people you let into your headspace and your heartspace, and that's a pretty sacred honor.

Chapter 24

SELF-CARE FOR WOMEN IN COMEDY

Now, I know you might read this chapter title and say to yourself, "Hey, I'm not a lady in comedy! This cannot possibly apply to me." But I'm pretty sure a lot of this advice applies to folks in various industries, especially folks of the woman variety. So give it a quick glance, and just replace the comedy references with stuff about making widgets or teaching children or running a factory. Okay? Cool. (And by the way, thanks to comedian and digital wizard Hilary Kissinger of the Upright Citizens Brigade Theatre for inspiring me to write this chapter.)

1. You have just as much a right to be in that room/on that stage/on that show/in that movie as any dude. In fact, you have more of a right, because you're a girl and you probably had to work harder to get there. (This goes triple for women of color, queer women, women with disabilities, women of size, or any women who aren't the "industry standard.") Remember this.

2. If people say "I don't usually find women funny, but you're great!" dismiss them as jerks, because they are jerks (except for the part about you being great, which is obviously true).
3. Take baths. They are soothing and relaxing. Just don't do this in California, because of the drought.
4. Get your own room on the road whenever possible. At least get your own couch. Tell people with whom you're touring that you like to take time for yourself. Go for a walk.
5. You can live like a pauper or on credit or off family donations or couch change or whatever until you're thirty-five, at which point I would like for you to buy some framed posters and stockpile quality tampons. Do everything else exactly as you've been doing it.
6. Invest in a great accountant.
7. You probably don't need a manager. If you are rich and famous you might need one. If you're trying to get sets at dive bars or go through the UCB system, focus on your work, not your management. You do need an agent, eventually.
8. Hire and fire people with grace. If they act like shitbags, treat them like children. If they act cool, act the same. Remember that you can like someone personally but not professionally, or vice versa.
9. Don't get caught up in what a lady blog thinks of you. They pay women a pittance (when they actually do pay women anything) to write lots of stuff. If somebody there likes your shit, great.

They were paid far less than they're worth to write said opinion. If they don't like you, fuck it. They were paid shit to write shit. You can revel in that knowledge or you can move on. Move on.

10. I was once asked what role I would like to play in a TV project based on my own life story. I said, "I kind of would like to write, but would that be weird for the other writers in the room? You know, because it's about me and stuff?" Diablo Cody looked at me and said, "If you were a man, would you ask me that question?" I remember that before every single meeting.
11. *Always ask for more.* More money. More credit. More wigs. Wigs are great. You can write off a portion of wigs on your taxes. I'm not kidding.
12. Don't drink, snort, smoke, or fuck everything. Most of the things: yes! All of the things: no! You must put your work first and that means being alive and healthy and reasonably sane.
13. Get enough sleep.
14. When in doubt, ask yourself what Amy Poehler would do.

Chapter 25

PRIORITIZE SLEEP

My friend used to work for the most terrible woman in New York. That's saying something, as New York is rife with terrible people. New York is also full of amazing people, the best humans on the planet! But in this case, we're talking about the most terrible woman in New York. She was terrible. Have I emphasized that enough? *Terrible.*

Everybody knew she was an awful boss. Everybody knew she made her employees unhappy. She regularly ran her staff ragged, playing favorites and ignoring complaints about supervisors who sexually harassed, intimidated, and frightened young women. She posited herself as a forward-thinking leader, but she treated everyone around her like shit. She expected them to work incredibly long hours for low pay, which is common enough in New York that most folks have learned to overlook it. They're just glad to have any job at all. She knew it, and she took advantage of that as much as she could. She never showed gratitude or praised anybody for a job well done. She turned on a dime—any day, one of her favorites could become fodder for the shark tank. She enjoyed making threats.

Never mind that her product sucked and she was more interested in fawning over her celebrity friends than in adequately compensating people for a job well done or in maintaining a healthy, cooperative office culture. She was in charge, and like any person gone mad from power, she had zero perspective on what the little people would need.

Occasionally, she would gather the staff together and talk in grand terms about work-life balance. I think this just meant she was gearing up for another long weekend in the Hamptons or something. At one point she got on a kick about the importance of sleep, which was highly entertaining to the rank and file, who got precious little sleep thanks to extra-long hours.

"Prioritize sleep," the boss said once. "If you sleep, you come to work rested. And then this company will stay on top."

My friend couldn't help herself. She snorted with laughter. The boss stared at her menacingly.

"What is funny?" the boss asked.

My friend thought fast.

"I just pictured my old boss talking to us like this," my friend said, shaking her head with awe. "He never would've cared enough to address the vital issue of sleep. Sometimes I can't believe how lucky I am to have landed here, with a boss who actually invests in the health of her employees. Do you know how rare that is?"

The boss swallowed the obvious bullshit and looked as proud as a peacock with impressive highlights.

"Yes," the boss said. "I do."

The other employees looked at my friend and rolled their eyes. When the boss wasn't looking, she mouthed, "Sorry."

When I heard the story, the only thing I could say when I was done laughing was, "That may have been the only intelligent point that woman has ever made."

We do need to prioritize sleep. It is vitally important. I think of it this way: My brain is a factory. When I sleep, the factory comes alive with activity, replenishing all the chemicals I need to get through my day. If I get eight to nine hours of good sleep, I wake up ready to kick ass and take names and then actually remember those names. If I don't give the factory the chance to do what it does best, I'm operating with a reduced supply of important fuel. I forget things. I bump into things. I yawn in the midst of important conversations. I'm quicker to anger. I'm quicker to sadness. I might develop a headache or get nauseated. I might even get quite anxious. I probably should not operate heavy machinery in such a state. Getting behind the wheel is a dicey proposition. Coffee can give me a jolt of energy, but the inevitable dive into the postcaffeine abyss can be quite painful.

Losing out on sleep is not only annoying, it's dangerous. We all know well the good ol'-fashioned American work ethic that says, "Keep going and going as hard as you can for as long as you can. Breaks are for pussies and Frenchmen!" Well, that kind of attitude is a surefire route to on-the-job accidents, car crashes, general crankiness, and other unsavory things.

You need sleep. You need a good amount of sleep. There is no honor in bragging that you can get by on five hours alone. Look, if you're a new parent or you work three jobs, I understand that sleep is precious and hard to get. But please do me a favor: if you engage in no other method of self-care, try to get a few good hours in when you can. Burning the midnight oil is fun until you burn right the fuck out. Trust me, I've done it. If you need to ask for a deadline extension, do it. If you need to set boundaries with your boss, or turn off your phone at night, do it. If you need to look for a new job that will actually allow you to rest like a healthy human, go for it. It's vital to your long-term health and well-being, and it'll make you a vastly more pleasant partner, coworker, parent, and human.

If you need tips on combating insomnia, I highly recommend a technique called the body scan. I learned it from the work of Jon Kabat-Zinn, who teaches it as a meditation technique—I recommend his work all the time, as in chapter 29 in this very book. He also gets a shout-out in chapter 2. Really, I'm a big fan. In the body scan, one lies on one's back in savasana, the corpse pose (spooky!), and practices breathing into each part of the body. It is really lovely to imagine sending glowing white light (or golden light, or rainbow glitter, or whatever you like) down to the toes, then to the ankles, then to the tops of the feet, and so on and so forth until you've reached the top of the head. The aim of the body scan meditation is to relax and feel refreshed. Personally, I fall asleep every damn time. It's wonderful for that! You can learn more about it in Jon Kabat-Zinn's book *Full Catastrophe Living.*

Other tips for better sleep: Spray your pillow with a mixture of lavender essential oil and water before you bed down for the night. Try a cup of soothing chamomile tea. Take a bath before bedtime. Shut off your electronic glowing screens at least fifteen minutes before you aim to fall asleep. Some folks like valerian root capsules before bed—they smell like ass but are allegedly quite effective. Of course, before you take any herbal supplement, check with your doctor for interactions with your regular prescriptions. You may also wish to listen to soothing relaxation music, or guided sleep recordings. There are plenty available online—I'm a particular fan of Belleruth Naparstek's work. I also like Tara Brach's podcast, which includes dharma talks and meditation exercises. I generally find it so soothing that I drift off to sleep partway through. It's not the aim of the podcast, but it's how I happen to enjoy using it. For me, it's cheaper than prescription sleeping medication, with fewer side effects.

I wish you the best on your journey to better sleep. I will see you in dreamland. (I mean, not really, that would be supercreepy and I wouldn't, like, invade your dreams without your consent—even if I had the power! But, you know, I mean, you know what I mean.)

Sweet dreams.

Chapter 26

SLEEP **NAKED**

If you're like most people, you don't absolutely love every single thing about your body. In fact, you might find some aspects of your body quite unfortunate, even revolting or deplorable. It makes me sad to say it, but body shame is a pretty common malady in our culture. And I've got a bit of an unconventional remedy.

Self-affirmations are great. Therapy is awesome. Cultural deprogramming is essential. But at the end of the day—and I mean that literally—the best thing I've ever done for my body image is to sleep naked.

We're often so disconnected from our bodies that it feels as if they are completely separate entities from our minds or spirits. This isn't true. It's all connected, which might explain why a case of the flu sometimes leaves you depressed and sad—or why a great run fills you with joy and elation. (Or so I've heard. I have yet to experience a great run, but whatever, I've heard stories.)

Sleeping naked is a great way to get to know your own body.

It's a fine method for getting in touch with your physical self. It's also quite comfortable, and you don't have to contend with being overheated by flannel pj's or annoyed by nocturnal underwear wedgies.

Try it. Run your fingers over your own skin and say hello. That's all. If you start to think thoughts like, *Oh, that is so gross* or, *Ew, I am so awful and unlovable,* please banish said thoughts. Or at least tell the critical voice inside you to be quiet for now. You're just saying hello. You may even be gently acknowledging and welcoming parts of yourself you've ignored for many years. That's a good thing. That's a kind thing. That's a part of self-care.

Locking the door is very helpful when you sleep naked. If that's not possible, keep a robe close by in case of emergencies. And if you sleep with somebody, they'd better be happy you've decided to start sleeping naked. If they're not, what the hell is their problem? They don't deserve to sleep with you, anyway. (Pets are exempt from this policy, as they rightly do not understand that not being naked is an option.)

Try it tonight. If you don't feel comfortable going all the way naked, try stripping down to your undies and sleeping that way. It's a wonderfully liberating and perfectly acceptable habit for a grown-ass adult. And it may just help you make peace with your own grown ass.

Chapter 27

ASK QUESTIONS

When I was a kid, I wanted to become a hard-hitting investigative journalist. I wanted to win a Pulitzer Prize, and I assumed I'd be rich, because reporters must obviously earn a lot of money. But the adulation and the income weren't the real reasons I wanted to be a journalist. No, I wanted to be Lady Woodward or Chick Bernstein for one main reason: the questions.

Reporters get to ask tons of questions that would be wildly inappropriate for normal citizens to ask. I've written a few cover stories for magazines—one on the luminous Lizzy Caplan, the other on the dynamite Laverne Cox, a third on the glorious Aidy Bryant—and it was so fun to ask them fangirl questions for my *job*. (Did you know Laverne likes to sing karaoke to blow off steam? Did you know Lizzy went to a performing arts high school in Los Angeles? Neither did I! Glad I asked!)

I'm nosy as hell and I'm a big fan of questions. I like to ask a bunch of them, one right after the other. If we ever meet in person, I'll probably sit you down, look you in the eye, and ask all sorts of things. Some of these questions may be inappropriate, and I'll be totally fine if you tell me you don't feel like answering me. I like to ask a lot of questions because I'm not supposed to ask a lot of questions. To question, then, is to rebel—politely and tactfully, with a smile.

Women aren't supposed to ask too many questions. If we do, we're annoying. Men aren't supposed to ask too many questions. If they do, they're weak. Men are supposed to just naturally know everything, and men who ask for help are just betraying their own giant dingle dangle dongles. Women are supposed to wait for men to explain everything. Women are not supposed to seek information on our own. If men don't think a thing is important enough for us to know, we should accept this and go back to, I don't know, crocheting doilies or baking cupcakes or reproducing (possibly all at the same time).

I find that asking questions is the best way to learn great stuff. Here are some of my favorite questions to ask new friends:

1. Where were you born?
2. Where did you grow up?
3. What is your number-one big career goal? (It is okay if you have more than one; I want to hear about those, too.)
4. What is your favorite flavor of ice cream?
5. What is your favorite building in the entire world, even if you haven't seen it in real life?
6. If you could have sex with any dead celebrity (while they were alive) who would you pick?

I also believe it's a good idea to ask questions of the friends you already know pretty damn well. Ask them how they are doing and if they are happy. Ask them how they really feel, not just how they think they should feel. Ask them questions that may have painful answers, so long as you truly need those answers.

I'll give you an example of the latter type of question. Recently, a pretty good buddy of mine came to town. I found out via social media. She's a busy bee and I know what it's like to show up for a trip and have folks who want to see you. You can't make everybody a top priority. But I wish she'd given me a heads-up, you know? It seemed odd that she hadn't. In addition, she'd been rather distant through our usual forms of communication for about a week. That may sound like a short period of time, and it is, in the grand scheme of things. But that coupled with the lack of notice about her trip made me wonder if something was up. Because I definitely would've let her know if I were in her town.

At first I sat with the uncomfortable feelings and the uncertainty. Then I said to myself, "Sara. This girl is your friend, or so you have been led to believe. Just ask her straight up if everything is cool. If it isn't cool, she'll let you know. If things are great, she'll reassure you she's just busy. And if she doesn't respond, she probably needs some distance from your friendship for whatever reason. Or she just sucks, because you are so awesome and she is missing out on serious unadulterated unfiltered amazingness!"

So I asked her. I could've called, but we don't talk on the phone, so that would feel strange. I could've texted, but she hadn't responded to texts in like a week (I wasn't texting a lot or anything—I guess I'd sent two texts over the course of a week with no response). So I shot her an email. For the purpose of this tale, I shall call her Barbra. Let us pretend she is Barbra Streisand.

Dear Barbra:

Hey, are we cool? I miss you. I know we're both really busy, but I wanted to check in just in case things weren't fine. I apologize if I'm being a silly goose. At any rate, I hope you're doing great.

XO,
Sara

Obviously a bit dorky and hardly the "too cool for school" approach I always dream of embodying, but at least I asked.

And then I waited.

And went about my day.

And kept living my life for a few days until I remembered she still hadn't gotten back to me.

Finally, it became apparent Barbra Streisand wasn't going to answer. And even though it hurt my feelings, I knew it was time to call it quits. I could've asked her for more information, but her silence told me all I needed to know. And besides, a great questioner knows when to stop asking questions.

I stopped questioning Babs, and, more important, I stopped questioning myself. Some of the questions I could've asked myself were: "Am I good enough? What did I do wrong? Am I an asshole? Am I a loser? How am I inadequate, and why do I definitely deserve this treatment?"

Once I'd come to peace with it, she actually emailed me back that she was totally fine, just superbusy. But by then I'd realized I needed to stop putting any effort into a friendship that was almost wholly one-sided.

I'm still glad I asked.

We should all ask more questions. Not just of our friends or ourselves, but of our bosses, our coworkers, our lovers, our acquaintances, our children. If you're at the doctor and you're confused about something, ask. Do not accept dismissive or brusque behavior. Yes, the doctor is busy; yes, he or she likely has only a few minutes to spend with you. But this is your body and your life and you deserve sufficient answers in a language you can understand. So ask. This is also true for the car mechanic; the teacher in charge of your child's welfare; the cab-driver; the flight attendant; or the zookeeper. Most people are happy to answer polite questions. They can't spend all day with you, but they can usually give you a few minutes.

I wish you many wonderful and fantastic questions and many equally amazing answers.

Chapter 28

SURPRISE!
YOU DON'T HAVE TO LOVE YOUR FAMILY

I have a friend who grew up with a pretty tough situation. A close male family member repeatedly raped her when she was a child. Finally, when she was twelve, she mustered up the courage to tell her mother about the years of abuse. This was the point at which her mother said, "I kind of thought something like that might be going on."

BUHSCUZE ME?

She "kind of thought" something "like that" was going on?

What a piece-of-shit human.

Bear in mind that I understand that the mother was likely enmeshed in a cycle of abuse and came from a background horrifying enough to lead her to believe such behavior was, if not appropriate, at least relatively common.

That being said, I honestly don't give a fuck. She didn't protect my friend, so she can fuck off into the sea. And as for the rapist, well, he's a monster who deserves horrible things I can't even begin to imagine. I have zero sympathy for him, regardless of what may have happened to him as a kid. I can understand something in context without accepting it, condoning it, or excusing it.

Here's how my friend's awful mother decided to deal with the situation. Did she call the cops? No. Did she bring my friend to a therapist? No. Did she even, at bare minimum, cut off all contact with the rapist? No. She merely decided that this male family member would never be permitted to have *unsupervised* visits with her daughter. Oh, he could still come over! He was still invited to Thanksgiving. He was still invited to Christmas. My friend was expected to be polite to him, to carry on a conversation with him, and to "dress appropriately" around him so, you know, she didn't tempt him into raping her child-body again, I guess.

Anyway, garbage logic from a garbage mother. The rapist is beyond garbage. I haven't figured out what to call him, exactly.

My friend and I are grown adults now. My friend is in her forties. She has been through many years of therapy. She's a badass and a tough cookie and a resilient woman, to say the very least. And her mother still expects her to show up at Thanksgiving and at Christmas and make nice with the now elderly and sick guy who traumatized her and made her childhood a horror show. At times it even seemed like her mother was going out of her way to force my friend into conversations with the rapist. Anything to keep things pleasant. Anything to keep up the pretense of a happy, healthy family.

My friend put up with it for years and years. At first, she didn't know any better. Then, when she got into therapy for post-traumatic stress disorder and suicidal depression, she came to understand that she put up with it because, among other things, she was terrified of losing a connection to the family members she did love. But it wore on her, year after year after year. Sometimes she figured she should just forgive him, especially when he became old and frail. And then finally, last year, she hit her limit. You know what she did?

She fired her mother.

When she told me about it, that's how she put it: "Oh, we're not going to their house for Thanksgiving this year. I fired my mother."

I was flabbergasted.

"You *fired* your *mother*?" I said.

"Oh yes," she said. "She's done a terrible job for years. Really should've fired her a long time ago."

Boy, was I impressed.

"I didn't even know somebody could do that," I said.

"I didn't, either," she said. "Then my therapist asked me if I'd ever considered it. I never had. It was awesome."

Not only did she fire her mother—she fired the other relatives who knew about the abuse. It didn't matter that they were all elderly—being old as hell doesn't excuse you for enabling brutality. She called them up and told them very calmly that their services would no longer be needed. She did not curse them out. She was not mean. Just as she'd rehearsed in her therapist's office, she was polite and professional, yet firm. She explained that they hadn't protected her when she was small, and they'd excused the rapist's criminal behavior. Lord knows how many other kids he tormented while folks looked the other way.

And as for him, well—she fired him a long time ago. The realization that she would never have to see him again was, she told me, a huge weight off her shoulders—as was the knowledge that he was too weak to hurt anybody else now.

When other family members asked her about it, she was very honest. Some of them didn't like it. Some of them shunned her. Others supported her. It's an evolving, ongoing thing. She has suffered for it at times and felt hurt and lonely. It's hard to know that even some of the supportive relatives still talk to her rapist. But she took her power back, and for the first time in a very long time, she feels free.

There are some folks who question my friend's decision—after all, her mother changed her diapers, fed her, kept her alive, went to her school events, even helped pay for her college. In many ways, she was a good mother. But she wasn't good enough. And as my friend knows very well from the corporate world, "not good enough" ain't gonna cut it in today's competitive job market.

Now, I know this is an extreme example. You may not be a victim of incest or physical or emotional abuse, and this story may not apply to your life. But I do think it's important to acknowledge something true: you are under no obligation to love your family.

This is a radical idea. It sounds heartless and cold and mean. I think it's a great idea, and it still sounds a little cruel to me when I say it out loud. But when you hear the sentiment behind it, it actually makes a lot of sense.

We do not choose our families. We are born into our families, or adopted into them, or otherwise placed in the care of individuals with more power than we have as little kids. We have no agency in the matter. And some of us get very lucky. We get the loving family with parents and grandparents and aunties and uncles and cousins all running around, happy and supportive and well fed and well loved. Sure, we don't always get along, and some of us would prefer not to hang around with one another too often, but we care about each other's welfare. We love each other, to one extent or another.

And then some folks aren't as lucky.

Some people have nightmare moms or horrible dads or mean grandparents. Some people have shitty cousins. Some people have entire families made up of assholes. I know more than one woman whose mother became enraged at her when she said, "Hey, your boyfriend is trying to have sex with me." I know guys whose fathers beat the shit out of them.

I'm not talking about relatives who go through tough times and can't be there for us in the way that we need. I'm not talking about distant but responsible fathers, cold but ultimately caring mothers, or siblings who just never quite click with us. I'm not talking about the petty jealousies and rivalries and dramas that arise in all families at some point in time.

I'm talking about abusers who never repent, apologize, or try to get help.

I'm talking about people who physically, mentally, or emotionally make you feel like shit, over and over and over again, and never ever make an effort to do things better.

I'm talking about people who genuinely hurt you, on purpose, repeatedly. Or who hurt you "by accident" but refuse to change when you point it out. They may say things like, "I'm sorry you feel that way, but that's just my way and I'm not gonna change." Then they hit the bottle again and call you up to tell you what a lazy piece of shit you always were. I've got news for you: that is no longer an accident.

You know what?

Fuck those people.

Fire them.

Get 'em out of your life.

If you can't cut them off completely for various reasons, well, know this: you do not have to love them. I mean it. You don't. Not even if they claim they love you. If your only possible act of rebellion against their bullshit is to look at them over the dinner table and say silently, inside your head, "I do not love you," well, hell, that sounds like a small but gorgeous victory to me.

Firing your family is not a decision to be taken lightly. I don't know anyone who *would* take it lightly. And if you fire only one particular family member, you're probably going to have to contend with other folks in the family who don't support you, or who do support you but who actually have a very nice relationship with that person. I would only suggest firing your family after long and careful deliberation in a professional therapist's office. And because we as humans naturally crave connection and affection, I'd advise you to look around at your friends and see if you can build a great family of your own. Maybe you've already done it without realizing it. You can't expect them to suddenly step in and be the mommy you always dreamed of or the sister you truly deserve. What you can hope for and encourage is the kind of open, loving relationship that happens when two adults who mostly have their shit together choose to hang out together, look after each other, and take care of each other.

When people treat you like garbage, they forfeit their right to be a part of your life. If it is possible to break ties with them, do that. Remember, you can still forgive them for their wrongdoings if you want to! Forgiveness can be beautiful and healing for the one who has been harmed, but it does not mean she is required to be BFFs with the person who hurt her. Forgiveness is a way of letting go.

You are a wonderful creature who deserves love and safety and happy companionship. I encourage you to seek out therapy and support from good folks, and to minimize your time with the jerks. Take very good care of you. Because you don't need to love your family, but you do need to love yourself.

Chapter 29

BREATHE

I could write a whole book about breathwork. I won't do it, because there are plenty of great guides already out there, and I want to encourage you to purchase as many books as possible in order to support your local independent bookstore. Also, other authors have done a fabulous job on this topic already, and I don't feel like trying to compete with the likes of Dr. Andrew Weil or Jon Kabat-Zinn (oy, that guy again, am I right?) or any of the rest. I'm not here to knock Pema Chodron off the meditation bestseller list. (At least that's what I want her to think. If I can lull her into a state of security, I can fucking own her ass.) Pema has her area of expertise in applying Buddhism to everyday life, and I've got my area of expertise in writing vagina jokes to alternately amuse and frighten strangers. We're both doing the Lord's work, in our own ways.

I first became aware of the concept of applied breathwork when I was but a wee tween in middle school. I'd go to the tobacco and comic book shop on Main Street (I don't know why these items were sold together, but the nineties were a different time) and I'd pick up a copy of *Sassy* magazine, a wonderful publication that distinguished itself from other teen publications by actually publishing good writing and by not talking down to its readership. *Sassy* was also noteworthy for alienating advertisers, but the world wasn't ready for it yet. Many of today's lady-blogs are direct descendants of *Sassy*. I mean, they put Kurt and Courtney on their cover, kissing. C'mon. That's badass.

One issue of *Sassy* (shit, or was it *YM*? Eh, doesn't matter now) had a little sidebar about a relaxation breath to relieve anxiety. It was called alternate nostril breathing. I've since learned it is used fairly frequently in yoga classes. It's rather embarrassing to do in front of people, but I found as an anxious kid that I could retreat to a bathroom stall during school hours or a mall trip and do alternate nostril breathing in private.

I advise you to be cautious with which breathing techniques you use at which times. It is possible to induce alternate states through breathwork and visualization. Trance and self-hypnosis are groovy and all, but you'll only want to do that after some good, solid training with a professional. In addition, if you are someone who experiences traumatic flashbacks, closing your eyes during breathwork may not feel safe. That is perfectly fine, because you will reap all the benefits of breathwork whether your eyes are open or closed. You've just got to keep bringing your attention back to your breath.

Anyway, alternate nostril breathing works like this: Close one nostril by pressing on it with a finger. Inhale through the other nostril for four even counts. Don't rush "onetwothree" and then take a pause and then count "four." You want steady counts: "One . . . two . . . three . . . four." Try to get the inhalation down into your belly, so it's not shallow breathing high in your chest but rather more full, diaphragmatic breathing. Now hold for seven even counts and switch your finger to press on the other nostril, freeing the previously blocked nostril. Breathe out of your newly free nostril for eight even counts. Pause for a moment or two. Then resume the cycle, inhaling through the free nostril for four, holding for seven, and exhaling through the other nostril for eight.

Weird, right? But kind of fun. And oddly relaxing, especially when you go through a few rounds of it gently, slowly, and quietly. The first round might be a bit ragged and weird, but you'll relax into it with each subsequent round.

It wasn't until years later that I learned that slow, even, deliberate breathing interrupts the body's natural fight-or-flight response and induces the relaxation response. You've experienced the fight-or-flight response any time you've had to hit the brakes hard in your car to avoid an accident. If you've ever been in an actual physical fight, your body naturally went into fight or flight. You probably didn't notice it, because it's automatic. The body perceives an outside threat and instantly prepares itself to fight or flee. Your quads tense up. Your arms usually get a bit tense, too. Your pupils dilate a bit to let in more light. Your body diverts blood flow from the extremities to your respiratory system and your cardiovascular system. Your breathing gets shallow, high in your chest. Your heart beats faster. Your adrenal glands release adrenaline. Stress hormones do their thing. You're in a state of physical arousal (and not the fun kind). In every way, your body is tensed for action.

This is an excellent response to have when threatened with real danger. But for many of us, the fight-or-flight response emerges when we run into triggering situations that are not actually life-threatening. There are many theories as to why some folks go into fight or flight on an airplane, or in the grocery store, or at the sight of an ex-boyfriend. If one associates abuse or pain with a trigger, it's understandable that one would have some kind of negative reaction. But when fight or flight kicks in, it's on another level. It can truly feel quite out of proportion to what's actually happening in the world around you. And there's a level of dissonance that creates mental confusion and sometimes great panic.

Panic attacks occur when the fight-or-flight response goes way out of control. It's as if your nervous system has overreacted and thrown a fit. In this case, you may feel nauseated, sweaty, shaky, and deeply afraid. It actually feels quite similar to that moment before you puke when you've got the stomach flu. You know the moment I mean. You're just desperate for the awful feeling to end. And when you puke, you get temporary relief. But with a panic attack, it's not so clear-cut. Panic attacks can go on for seconds, minutes, or even hours. They're usually pretty short, but they can wipe you out and leave you feeling exhausted.

In some folks, the symptoms of a panic attack are not unlike the symptoms of a heart attack. If you've never experienced a panic attack before, your first one can leave you convinced you are dying. In earlier generations of my family, some folks would end up in the emergency room for this reason. They'd be sent home with a nice sedative or a recommendation to take more naps. Ah, the good old days. (As an aside, when folks say, "What era do you wish you were born in?" I always say, "Um, I'm a queer woman with mental illness. I'll stay right the fuck here, right the fuck now, thank you very much.") Anyway, if you're experiencing frightening and unusual symptoms, by all means, get your ass to a doctor. It is much better to be stuck with an ER bill for a panic attack than to die because you told yourself a heart attack was "just in your head." (Neither a panic attack nor a heart attack is "just in your head," but only one can kill you.)

When doctors used to talk about "the vapors" and prescribe smelling salts and soothing baths, they were sometimes talking about panic attacks. "Hysteria" was a catchall term for the emotional and psychological troubles of women, and a woman in the throes of a panic attack could easily be described as "hysterical." Men could be hysterical, too, but the term had a distinctly feminine connotation. Besides, men were encouraged to drink away their troubles, or go shoot something or punch something. I have seen men deal with panic attacks through anger. Anger is an active emotion. It feels empowering. It's also a distraction from fear. This is not to say that women don't attempt to use rage to escape fear. But we still tend to look at the woman as the one who calms the man down, not the other way around. Women aren't socialized to express anger. We're taught to internalize it, keep it inside, stuff it down, and pretend everything is great. No wonder more women report panic attacks than do men.

Anyway, breathwork is an excellent way to interrupt the fight-or-flight response. It slows down your rate of respiration. It slows down your heart rate. It soothes you. It relaxes you. There are endless breathing techniques out there, some best used in combination with specific visualization exercises. I'm just sharing the ones that I find useful.

If that first technique sounded confusing or bizarre, have no fear. I'm a big fan of the 4-7-8 breath without alternate nostril breathing, too. You can do it by inhaling for four even counts, holding for seven even counts, and exhaling for eight even counts. Then you repeat as often as you like. Some people prefer this to the alternate nostril breathing; others really like the fact that alternate nostril breathing has a kind of extra physical trick to require you to focus. If I'm driving and dealing with high anxiety or even a panic attack, I only do the alternate nostril breathing if I can pull off the road and safely rest somewhere. If I must proceed in traffic, I'll do the regular 4-7-8 breath. For some reason, I find the alternate nostril breathing induces a bit more of a pleasantly loopy state after a few rounds. That's a lovely feeling, but not one I wish to have while driving. With the regular 4-7-8 breath, I feel more alert and focused, though still relaxed.

If you have a good friend or loved one with you, you may wish to ask them to hold your hand and even do the breathing with you. That may feel safer than doing it alone. I remember once asking a chaperone on a school trip to breathe with me as I attempted to talk myself down from a horrible panic attack. She didn't know what the hell I was talking about. If I had more experience with it, I would've felt able to do it on my own.

Don't just reach for the breathing techniques when you're at the height of anxiety. Practice your breathing techniques when you're feeling calm, too. It's sort of like working out at the gym in preparation for the eventual athletic competition or marathon. You've got to keep up with your training. Breathing techniques will *always* help you at least a little bit, but they'll help you more if you do them regularly and associate them with comfort, relaxation, and calm. It's also interesting to see how chilled out you get when you start from a baseline of feeling "normal," whatever that means to you. Sometimes you go into a really lovely, floaty state. When you're in a state of high anxiety and do a familiar breathwork technique, you may find it simply takes you down to "normal" rather than some kind of chill hippie state. Interestingly enough, this was also my experience taking the drug Xanax. If I took it while feeling perfectly fine, it would induce a kind of dopey feeling. But if I took it when I was having a panic attack, it would simply bring me down to normal.

Anyway, breathwork is cheaper than Xanax and available without a prescription. I'm a big fan of the integrative approach to medicine, where you combine conventional medicine (like, say, Xanax) with alternative medicine (like, say, therapeutic massage or acupuncture or applied breathwork). It's empowering because it gives you options. You're not dependent on one magical cure. You've got a whole host of magical cures on reserve. Also, breathwork is not addictive. It is neither habit-forming nor harmful to your health, your relationships, or your work. You can do it anywhere, at any time. You can even do it while you're making a presentation at work or standing in front of the altar to get hitched or, I don't know, walking on hot coals at some inspirational seminar. To me, these sound like equally pleasant scenarios.

And breathwork isn't just for people diagnosed with severe anxiety or panic attacks. It's for everybody! It can help you clear your mind, focus on the task at hand, and accomplish your goals. It can also help you fall asleep at night. It can be invigorating or relaxing, or both all at once. Athletes have long known the power of breath to change their bodies and mental states. Buddhist monks know it, too. In fact, many of the breathing techniques I've learned were actually developed by meditating monks.

I strongly encourage you to check out *Full Catastrophe Living* by Jon Kabat-Zinn. Learn more about mindfulness meditation and breathwork there. There are many, many other books that cover this subject in depth, but that one is my all-time favorite. Kabat-Zinn makes the distinction between meditation and relaxation in a far more elegant way than I can. Suffice it to say that meditation techniques are better used in the morning or at midday, while relaxation techniques are better used at night, when one wishes to induce sleep.

Careful, slow, applied breathwork has saved my life and my sanity many times over. I hope you never require anything so dramatic, and that you simply use these techniques to get a good night's rest or to pass the time at the DMV.

Also—and I'm not going to get into this, because my parents are going to read this—breathwork can totally enhance your sex life. I don't know a thing about Tantra, but I do know it's got to do with breathwork and energy and—hell, I don't know. Just go ask Sting. He'll know. (Boy, will he ever.)

Chapter 30

GIVE **IT** AWAY **NOW**

I lived in California full-time for two years, just long enough to get used to it. For the first year, I lived in a magical pink cottage in Highland Park on the property of a lovely gal named Susan. Susan's home was surrounded by birds and butterflies and greenery and Japanese lanterns and wandering kitty cats and adorable dogs. For the second year, I lived in a spacious two-bedroom apartment in Toluca Lake. It was a nice building and the neighborhood was very pretty. We could walk to Trader Joe's and a variety of cute shops, as well as Bob's Big Boy and the legendary Smokehouse. We even got our own little puppy, who promptly ruined the wall-to-wall carpeting. She was adorable and it was totally worth the money we had to pay to replace it when we moved out.

We moved out of the apartment because we decided to move back to New York so that my gentleman-caller-at-the-time could take a job there. As a writer of books and other things, my work is fairly portable. I couldn't see fit to stay in Los Angeles when I could easily move with him to Brooklyn and schlep back and forth if necessary for the development of film and TV projects and other moneymaking schemes that might arise, like investing in kale futures or gambling on extreme yoga competitions. I do love Los Angeles very much, and I knew I was going to miss living there full-time, so I had a couple of big-ass parties to say a temporary good-bye to my friends. One of these parties was a giveaway party.

I love giveaway parties! They're easy to throw, loads of fun, and quite useful. Here's how they work: you walk around your house and gather up all the stuff you don't want but that might prove useful or amusing to someone else. If you've been following my Purgatory Bag method from chapter 6, you may have decided that some objects shouldn't be thrown out or put away but rather ought to be given away. Brilliant! Put all of the giveaway things in one corner of your house.

Now here's the fun part. Send an invitation to people you really like, people you sort of like, and people you can stand for a couple of hours. Make the invitation say something like this:

> *Hey there, person who likes stuff! I'm having a giveaway party at my house with all kinds of useful items! And I'll give the stuff away for free (yes, FREE) so long as you agree to bring something to share (booze, snacks, whatever) and you agree to haul the stuff away yourself. Bring a bag! Bring multiple bags! And read below to see an itemized list of everything I'll have on offer.*

You can make a list of everything you might give away. You can even have some fun with the descriptions or list what you think the monetary value would be if you were to actually sell it at a garage sale. People might not show up for a footstool, but they might show up for "IKEA footstool from 2014, originally priced at $50, in mint condition." For extra zazz and sparkle, you can take photos and attach them to the email (I assume it's an email, and not a formal paper invitation, but perhaps you are Amish).

Arrange the objects in an attractive manner in a part of your house. If you're giving away loads of furniture, be sure to clearly label or tag the giveaway objects so that you don't find people trying to haul away your favorite armoire filled with all your sex toys. Regardless, you must clearly delineate the "shopping" areas, or else people will ask you if it's cool if they take that package of Q-tips in your bathroom. Then set up a bar and a snack table near the shopping area, and you're good to go!

Some people will ask me, "Sara, why don't you just sell the stuff on Craigslist or donate it to a charity that comes and picks up all the stuff for free?" These are excellent options, and I don't seek to dissuade you from either one! I just find that it's a bit more fun when your old wooden rocking horse goes to somebody you know. And if you're like me and have a bunch of friends who are into thrift stores and garage sales, this will feel like an awesome treasure hunt to them. Plus, they'll take some of your odd stuff that a charity might not want. What kind of odd stuff? I don't know! I don't know what kind of freaky shit you possess! That's your business. I'm just telling you, one of your buddies or acquaintances will probably dig it.

Ultimately, a giveaway party is a fun way to get to see some pals, have a chat, share some laughs, and then trick them into cleaning your house for you. Everybody wins! Note: If you get people slightly intoxicated, they are more likely to take more stuff. Just a hint—but you didn't hear that from me.

Chapter 31

ABUSE IS **FUCKING** COMPLICATED

Once upon a time, I did my friend Dave's podcast. Dave's a great guy, handsome and smart and funny, with a boatload of anxieties. He's very open about them, and he talks about that stuff onstage and on his podcast. The premise was that I would come in and talk about the event that had scared me the most in the world. Before I got to the studio, I decided I would talk about agoraphobia and panic attacks, subjects with which I am intimately familiar. I told Dave as much in advance. And then when I actually got to the studio and sat down with Dave, we chitchatted a bit, shot the shit, enjoyed ourselves. Finally, Dave asked me what the scariest experience in my life had been, and I opened my mouth to talk about panic attacks. What came out was something to the effect of "One time this guy hit me in the face."

I was as surprised as Dave. Neither of us had planned on that story coming out. To be fair, Dave didn't even know there was a story of that nature in my life. And because I had long pretended that incident hadn't happened, I was particularly taken aback by my apparent need to discuss the event.

I then proceeded to minimize the experience as best I could: "It didn't leave a bruise . . ." "I don't want to pretend it was as bad as it gets for other people who *really* get abused . . ." "I think he's a good person and just made a mistake . . ." "He was black-out drunk and he didn't believe me when I told him about it the next day, so I guess it didn't really happen for him . . ."

I remember Dave asking me, "Why are you making this smaller than it is? Why are you making excuses for this person?" and I think I said, "I don't know." I'm approximating my answers here, because I've never gone back and listened to that episode of the show. I find the prospect upsetting. Also, I didn't tell anyone else that I'd spoken about it—I left the studio and promptly pretended *that* hadn't happened, either. So imagine their surprise when it came out and random people approached them in person or on the Internet to say things like, "Wow, your friend is so brave" and also "So who was that guy?"

At this juncture, I should perhaps explain the following: It was a long time ago. He was not my boyfriend. We were seeing each other even though he hated to use that term ("dating" was another big no-no). We were sleeping together. We were also sleeping with other people, or at least those were the rules that had been set up. Anyway, he found out I'd slept with somebody else, went into a blackout drunk rage, and as we fell asleep (I thought we were falling asleep), he smacked me. Then I tried to leave and he held me down. Ten minutes after he smacked me, I said something to the effect of "I did not like that" and he said, "Did not like what?" I said, "You smacked me." He said,

"No I didn't!" He sounded genuinely astonished. I realized then that he was passing out in between bouts of calling me a slut or saying hateful things about whatever dude I'd hooked up with. I think he really didn't remember hitting me.

I stayed for the following reasons:

1. After he forcibly restrained me, I figured it was best to just sit tight.
2. I didn't want anybody else in the house to hear what was going on, because I didn't want to embarrass him.
3. I was humiliated and thought I deserved his rage (though not the smack; that seemed uncalled for) because I had exercised the nonmonogamous clause in our nonmonogamous relationship. I must be a slut for doing that. He said I was, and I liked him, so it must be true.
4. It was raining really hard and I told myself it would be really hard to get a cab in that weather. (This was obviously a bullshit excuse, but Uber hadn't been invented yet, and I was really afraid that if I left he wouldn't date me anymore. Not that I was allowed to use the term "dating" with him in the first place.)

At this point, some people who know me are reading this and going, "Who the fuck is this motherfucker? I'll kick his fucking ass!" And some people who don't know me are reading this and going, "What a piece of shit. I want to write him hate mail." You should know the following:

1. I did not break things off with him at that point. I was just so glad somebody wanted to hang out with me on a regular basis. Plus, he never did it again, so I figured, we all make mistakes.
2. I forgave him. Sort of. I guess. Well, I tried to, anyway. We all do terrible shit sometimes. Once I smacked a boyfriend for making a fat joke about me. That was a bad thing to do. So I can't sit on my high horse and pretend I'm an angel.
3. I am not going to tell you his name.

   Why? Because it would make life harder for me. And after a lifetime of getting in my own way, I am no longer interested in making life harder for myself than is absolutely necessary.

Here's what would happen if I named the guy:

1. He'd deny it. Remember, he doesn't remember what happened. Or he claims he doesn't remember what happened.
2. Some of my friends and/or readers and/or well-meaning Twitter followers would contact him and call him a piece of shit. They'd threaten him and say mean things. I have friends with massive Twitter followings, and every once in a while one of them will go in on somebody—a troll, a hater, whatever. What happens then is that their army of yes-men also goes in on the object of their rage. The problem is that the object of their rage is a human being with thoughts and

feelings. Now, if the object of rage is some douchebag with an egg icon (the default Twitter icon when you don't upload a photo) spewing racial epithets and acting like an asshole, I don't feel bad about what they deal with. But there are legions of fanboys and fangirls (and I say this as a fan) who are raring to go, ready to fuck up anybody (*especially a woman*) who dares say a bad word about their friend or idol. A lot of folks who go in on people on Twitter will later say, "But it's not *my* fault my followers threatened to beat up/humiliate/rape/kill the person I criticized. I can't control my followers." Exactly, you can't control your followers, so it's on you to recognize your own power in the situation and back off. Bite your tongue so hard it bleeds if necessary.

3. People would choose sides. I don't want that.
4. My life would get awkward for a while. I'm awkward enough as it is.
5. He might threaten me.
6. Somebody would say I was lying. And because nobody else was there in that room with us, nobody would be able to say for certain whether I was lying or he was lying. (Hi, I'm not lying about this.)
7. I would feel humiliated all over again, traumatized and embarrassed and guilty for letting it happen and for dragging his name through the mud.
8. Someone would write a think piece on the Internet. As I prefer to be the person who writes the think pieces rather than the person about whom the think pieces are written, this prospect does not excite me.

9. People who love me would get very, very upset.
10. People who love him would get very, very upset.
11. Every statement I've ever made would be up for trial in the court of public opinion. Am I a liar? Am I a bitch? Am I a bad person? What about that one time when I treated that person like shit? What about the times I've lied, and cheated, and acted like an asshole? Don't those times mean I'm not allowed to cast the first stone?
12. Ultimately, it would hurt me way more than it would hurt him. You know why? Because I'm a woman.

If you think I'm exaggerating about that last bit, consider the women who've accused Bill Cosby of raping them. How many folks have accused these women of lying for money or attention—even the gals who have plenty of money of their own and have made it clear they're not in it for the cash? And there are so many of those women, with such similar stories. I'm just one girl who says a guy smacked her one rainy night. Whoop-de-doo, right?

Wrong.

What I realized after doing Dave's podcast (and dealing with the fallout from it) is that when I minimize my own experience, I'm minimizing the experiences of other women who've dealt with the same thing (or much worse). It's okay that the guy smacked me, because he was drunk. It's okay that he held me down, because while he was doing it he was saying, "Don't go," in this kind of vulnerable way and it must've been because he really *liked* me, right? When I say, "Getting smacked is not a big deal," what I'm really saying is, "I will tolerate this behavior, and you should, too."

There is a place between black and white where reality exists. It's an uncomfortable place, but it's where I'm sitting right now, as I tell you this story.

I have a famous friend who told a story in public about a well-known individual who did something creepy. Not criminal; not abusive; not intimidating; just creepy. Yucky. Icky. Unseemly. She did not say his name, but people jumped on it and freaked out about it, trying to figure out who the fellow was. They made her life a bit of a nightmare for a few days, trying to figure out who this guy was and what exactly he'd done. But she didn't talk about it to get him in trouble, or to become some warrior woman for the legions of women who've been creeped out by gross dudes. She told the story because it was her story to tell, and she had a point to make, and that point was not, "Hey everybody, let's rake ________ over the coals!" Press started hitting her up, and her response was a rather more colorful version of "Um, get away from me, please."

There is a difference between trashing someone's reputation for sport and telling one's own truth.

Here's my truth: It took me years and years to admit that thing happened to me. Once I did (in a typically rather public fashion), I went to therapy to deal with it. I dealt with it. I'm writing about it, and I suppose that is another strategy for dealing with it: bringing it into the light, looking thoughtfully and even critically at my own reaction. It was a trauma, and I do myself and the reader no good service by pretending otherwise. At this point, the man in the story is nearly inconsequential, because

I'm not interested in what he thinks or feels. I'm interested in critically interrogating my own reaction to the event as well as my reaction to the reactions to the event. And, as ever, I'm interested in making other folks feel less alone.

While I am all for holding people accountable, I want you to know that you do not have to name names. You do not have to be the warrior princess (or prince, or nonbinary individual of royal status) who slays the dragon of abuse/prejudice/ignorance/whatever. You do not have to be anybody's icon or anybody's tower of strength. You get to be you, flawed and fucked-up and scared and imperfect.

I do think you should talk about it. I do think you should tell people who understand you, or who seek to understand you, if that feels comfortable to you. I do think you should sit in your power, own your truth, and free yourself of fear that your past is your future.

If your situation compels you to name names, do it. I'm not telling you to hide something or shy away from seeking justice for injury of the emotional or physical sort.

And if none of this sounds palatable and you don't like the way I handled my situation? That's fine. I'm not the boss of you. Your friends aren't the boss of you. Your family isn't the boss of you. Your abuser isn't the boss of you. You are the boss of you, and part of taking ownership of your own life is taking ownership of your own narrative.

I guess that's what I just finally did.

Chapter 32

MAKE ART LIKE A LITTLE KID

When I was twenty-nine years old, I got laid off from a job in the entertainment industry in beautiful New York City. The news came as a relief, although of course there were other emotions, too—fear, disappointment, anger, hurt, resentment. Mostly I was just glad I never had to work at that place ever again. I knew I'd miss a couple of people, and I kept in touch with those people. Today, we have all blessedly escaped and moved on to better careers. Good glory, was it a relief to get the hell out. I have never seen so many people scrambling so desperately for so little. The place was packed with bleeding, inflamed assholes whose highest aspiration in life was to give away free Creed tickets or to personally interview the third-runner-up of *The Bachelorette*.

After my layoff, I had a lot of free time on my hands. I got a decent going-away package, which meant I didn't have to worry about money for a little while. Instead of immediately beginning to look for new work, I decided I would first develop a new hobby.

I'm not sure what drew me to collage. Maybe it was the fact that I cannot draw a damn thing to save my life. Nor can I sculpt or paint or carve or whittle or do any of those wonderful things. I admire visual artists so very much for their ability to make incredibly beautiful things out of disparate elements. It is an absolute marvel to me to see someone turn a block of clay into a smooth, gorgeous vessel.

Anyway, cutting up magazines and various books and junk mail and combining it with glue and paint and glitter and markers? It sounded like a hell of a lot of fun. I used to love doing that way back in high school, so why not now, as I teetered on the edge of thirty? Perhaps it would be therapeutic.

My boyfriend kept telling me to mourn the loss of my job, to really go through all the stages that Elisabeth Kübler-Ross discussed. He told me that a job loss is a huge stressor even if you were glad to get out, even if every day was incredibly stressful. He said to deal with the layoff. You know, feel all the feelings. But at that point I was still very much into stuffing all the feelings down, at least when it came to work. So instead, I found art. I went to the art store and got me some paper and some paints, and I started making stuff. Nothing beautiful, mind you, but I liked the way the paint smelled and I liked splashing it around the paper.

My boyfriend cautiously got on board, as he hoped I might perhaps be engaging in some kind of self-directed art therapy. He bought me a bunch of awesome stamps and stamp pads. I spent money I didn't have on all kinds of scrapbooking and collage items from Etsy. And then I tried to sell impish, kitschy greeting cards on Etsy, which ended once I realized it would take actual effort for me to fulfill orders. I think that's when I finally descended into depression and started feeling all the feelings.

Anyway, I hold fast to my belief that my initial instincts were correct. Making art like a kid can be really fun! If only I hadn't tried to adultify it and turn it into a business, I think I would've had a very nice time with my paints and glue and glitter and construction paper and all the rest. If I hadn't pushed past the playful aspect and tried to make it a new cottage industry, well, I might've eventually broken through to a place where I felt able to safely deal with the feelings about the job.

Years later, I've developed some good habits with regard to art as stress relief. When I'm feeling particularly jammed or stopped up creatively or personally, I go to the store and buy construction paper and some crayons or glitter pens, whatever strikes my fancy. I don't get high-quality shit. I don't order the pricey stuff online. I grab what's on hand at the store, the way you might for a kindergartner on a rainy day. Then I go home and go to town. I draw whatever I want, as poorly as I want. I don't try to do a great job. I don't try to be good at art. I don't try to create anything remotely resembling a masterwork. I create art like a little kid, joyfully and freely. I put on some pop music and forget about life for a while. Sometimes I scribble in time with the music. Sometimes I end up putting the drawings on the fridge until I get tired of looking at them. I always enjoy myself. I always find some relief in the mere action of holding a tool in my hand and using it to express a feeling.

I do not create great art. But then, it's not for anyone else but me.

If you are also a member of the can't-even-draw-a-decent-stick-figure club, I invite you to try making art like a little kid. If you're feeling low-budget, do what I do and hit up Walgreens. If you're feeling blessed with abundance, by all means, go to an art supply store and wander around. Feel the different types of paper and canvas. Look at the brushes as if you know what the hell that weird fan-shaped one is for. Refuse to be cowed by the presence of "actual" artists. You are an artist, too, remember? Buy oil pastels. They're messy and great. Buy some paper. Go home and go to town. I promise that if you send me photos of what you make, I will always applaud your effort and tell you that you are as gifted as Michelangelo. And you won't even care that I'm teasing you, because you know that I know that it's not about being *good*—it's about being free.

Chapter 33

BRIDGE THE GAPS IN **YOUR** POP **CULTURAL** EDUCATION

As we've established, I was not a cool kid. I spent a lot of time by myself, inventing worlds in my mind. My parents were not hip parents, which is to say they weren't up on the hot new trends in parenting, or in children's toys and entertainment. Sure, I got a Cabbage Patch doll when they were popular, but that's only because I also got a little brother and I wanted some kind of reward to soothe the ache of giving up the coveted only-child position. (And by the way, Mom and Dad, you were very cool in all the important ways, like the "paying for me to go to a psychiatrist" way and the "feeding me and clothing me and loving me" way.)

But really, I could have been more determined. I read all the time, assisted in this pastime by the fact that my mother was a children's librarian. I thought authors were rock stars and books were the most coveted must-have items of any season. Why would I waste time watching *The NeverEnding Story* when I could *write* a never-ending story of my own and force my parents and grandmother to read it? Why would I spend an hour and a half on *Labyrinth* when I could spend *six* hours holed up in my bedroom making my dolls act out elaborate tableaux that would've put any telenovela to shame? Later, when everyone began binge-watching things, I claimed I didn't have time to binge-watch anything; I was too busy coming up with ideas for television shows that other people would want to binge-watch.

I conveniently ignored the fact that in order to create something awesome, you've got to know the history of the genre. You've got to know the context in which you are creating said awesome thing. You are never going to just waltz in and reinvent the wheel. I don't care how good you are; you're not *that* good. You've got to have sufficient respect for other creators who've plied your trade.

If you're a revolutionary, you've got to know what rules you're going to upend with your passionate rhetoric and wild ideals. Otherwise, you'll end up in the ice cream shop yelling, "It is time to combine chocolate with vanilla!" while everybody else happily licks their chocolate-vanilla swirl sundaes and pities your lack of knowledge (or, worse, laughs at your hubris).

It is time for us to take a careful accounting of our own pop cultural blind spots and embrace the things we have thus far ignored, rejected, or simply missed. Because I am the author of this book, I will start. Here are the things I have never listened to, watched, learned, or otherwise experienced:

1. *Raiders of the Lost Ark* (except for the scene in which the Nazi's face melts)
2. Most of the Harry Potter films (although I really enjoyed *Goblet of Fire,* which I call *Gobz of Fuego*)

3. Any *Rambo* film
4. A few Pixar hits
5. *Arrested Development* (the show; I was all about the band)
6. *Entourage* (I feel fine about this and will not be remedying it anytime soon, as I think it is *Sex and the City* for dudebros. Incidentally, yes, I have seen nearly every episode of *Sex and the City*.)
7. A lot of the latter episodes of *Full House*
8. Much of *Boy Meets World* and its subsequent reboot
9. Much of *Star Trek: The Next Generation* (and yes, I plan to rectify this)
10. The multiseason hit reality show *Big Brother*
11. The multiseason hit reality show *The Bachelor* and/or *The Bachelorette*
12. The fine documentary program *Keeping Up with the Kardashians*
13. Most things Errol Morris has made
14. Most things the late, great John Candy made
15. The vast majority of old and new *Degrassi*
16. A lot of Spielberg's stuff
17. Probably everything else you've ever watched or loved

I'm working on it, though! Just last July Fourth, I watched *Rocky*. It was great! I caught about 30 percent of Stallone's dialogue, but man, what a story! It's basically a fairy tale about fucking the social anxiety disorder right out of a proto-hipster, turning her into a fashionable gal about town. It is also a manifesto on black excellence and subverting the paradigm of white supremacy as expressed through our cherished but hollow patriotic myths and symbols. Did Howard Zinn watch *Rocky*? I bet he loved it! I love it! And now, because I am by nature evangelical about my precious few pop cultural obsessions, I want everybody else to love *Rocky*, too.

I wish you the best of luck in your pop culture education. Go out there and watch all the stuff your parents ignored or wouldn't let you watch. Have a great time! I promise that no matter how popular the thing you missed is, I totally understand why you might have missed it and I pledge to never, ever make fun of you for it.

Unless you haven't seen *Star Wars*. In which case, what in the actual fuck? Were you born in a charmless Hell-pit devoid of fun? I pity you, I really do.

Chapter 34

WHEN PEOPLE **TELL** YOU **WHO** THEY **ARE, BELIEVE THEM**

Most women who date men have a story that goes something like this: "I met this great guy and he was so funny and cute and sexy. He told me right away that he wasn't ready for anything serious, but I figured that was just because he hadn't met *me* yet. I was so nice to him and so supportive and great and we had sex and I met his friends and we went on the best dates. Then I found out he was fucking somebody else. It was the worst."

Well, yes, it was the worst. It sucked. And yes, he probably could have been clearer with you, like this: "I'm seeing different people and I think you should know that." But in the end, there's no one to blame, because *he told you who he was when he met you*. You just didn't believe him, because you didn't want to believe him. But as the great Maya Angelou once said, "When someone shows you who they are, believe them the first time."

I know it hurts. I've been there. Sometimes, if I'm brutally honest, this is about my own ego: "But I'm so amazing! Of course he'll give up fucking other women in order to fall deeply and wholly in love with me, me, me! This is how great and powerful I am! I have decided I need this person to love me in order for me to be okay!"

Now, there are some folks in this world who are just liars. They're assholes and thieves and jerks. They'll tell you anything you want to hear, just to fuck you or fuck *with* you. But most people will give you at least a hint of who they are within the first few hours of your meeting. Your job is not to be a detective (unless that is, in fact, your job—haaaay, Mariska Hargitay!) but simply to keep your eyes and ears and heart open to receive information.

If he doesn't answer your texts? That's information. If he doesn't answer your calls? That's information. If he cancels on you repeatedly? That's information.

This isn't just about heterosexual relationships, of course. It's about any relationship. If your boss repeatedly tells you there's a promotion coming your way, and it never materializes? That's information. If your coworker says he's going to help out with a project and he consistently fails to do so? That's information. If your dear friend says, "I love you so much!" and then ignores your birthday or your plea for advice? That's information.

It's rare that a person walks right up to you and says, "Hi. I am a sociopath" or "Hi. I am a pathological liar" or "Hi. I am the living, breathing human equivalent of a douchebag." Sometimes they tell you who they are through their actions. You've got to stick around a little while to figure the puzzle out.

I have a friend whose sister constantly makes up lies. She's been lying since the day she was born. My friend knows it. Her parents refuse to accept it. But my friend accepted it a long time ago. Oddly enough, her sister told her who she was by telling her a series of falsehoods. My friend got to know her sister very early on when she caught her in many lies. She doesn't think her sister can help it—it's that ingrained. It's that deep. But she doesn't make excuses for her sister, either. She simply uses the information to proceed in a way that is safer and healthier. She maintains a distance from her sister. She communicates with her only when absolutely necessary. Her sister isn't going to change, and my friend knows it in her bones.

Sometimes a new friend will express surprise when he or she hears that I wrote a book about panic attacks.

"But you seem so chill," they'll say. "You're so fun-loving and carefree and uninhibited."

I used to love that compliment. I still do, actually! But I quickly knock it right down, because if we're going to be real friends, these folks need to know what they're getting into.

"Thank you," I'll say. "But I'm really not. I take a lot of medication and I go to therapy. Some days I have a lot of trouble leaving my house. I'm afraid of a lot of things. Sometimes it's hard and sometimes it's easy. These days are pretty good, mostly. But it flares up."

While I believe that one should take a compliment, one also needs to be honest about oneself when one can.

In the interest of practicing this habit, I shall now present to you a list of true things about me. I'm going to tell you exactly who I am.

1. I am very loving.
2. I am not very clean.
3. I care a lot about other people.

4. I am self-centered.
5. I like to help strangers out.
6. I make promises on which I sometimes cannot deliver, though I earnestly mean to do so.
7. I'm usually late.
8. I thrive best in an independent work environment.
9. I really think I have the best job(s) in the world. This does not stop me from complaining about said job(s).
10. I have lied, cheated, and stolen.
11. I have a deep-seated mean streak that emerges on occasion, and I try to tell myself I'm using my meanness for good, but I'm usually just being a shithead.
12. I'm trying to be a better person and I'm pretty sure that even when I die, I won't be done with that.

If you could tell people twelve important things about you, what would these things be? What would you reveal and what would you conceal? Try writing this list down on a piece of paper. You can always tear that piece of paper up and flush it down the toilet (or, better yet, recycle it). I suggest you balance out the more negative items with the more positive items. It's an interesting exercise, and a neat way to get to know yourself better. You may actually find you don't want to throw the paper out, but wish to share it with somebody else.

Oh, and by the way? If anybody ever says to you, "I'm the best guy in the world!" he just did you a favor. What he's actually saying is, "I am an actual demon person who should be avoided at all costs." Do not date him, ever.

Chapter 35

ASK FOR **EXACTLY** WHAT **YOU WANT**

"I think I'm really good at my job, so, like, I guess more money would be cool."

Unconvincing.

"Over the past year, I've increased our sales by twenty-five percent. I received a glowing performance review from my supervisor. I've brought valuable clients into the company. I love working here and I'm eager to continue the progress I've already made. I think this merits a raise, and I would love to discuss that further with you."

Far more convincing!

It took me a long time to learn that I should ask for exactly what I want. Sure, I might have to back that up with specific reasons that justify why I should have what I want. And yes, it's true that the mere act of asking does not guarantee the reward I seek. And yet I maintain that I should ask for it all the same.

I used to tiptoe around asking for exactly what I wanted. I never wanted to bother anybody. Never wanted to put anybody out. Never wanted to risk disapproval or dismissal or disinterest.

"Would it be okay if . . ."

"I know this is so stupid, but . . ."

"You totally don't have to say yes, but . . ."

"I'm so sorry to ask, but . . ."

That kind of thing. Always with the qualifiers, the excuses, the apologies.

In order for you to ask for exactly what you want, you have to believe that you deserve it. You have to believe that you've earned it, by work or by simple virtue of existence. And many of us grow up thinking we don't deserve much, or that we shouldn't expect anything great. We think we're not worth it. We think we're not good enough. We think that the act of asking is an act of hubris.

I see this in particular with some of my women friends. Sometimes they'll resist self-promotion because they don't want to appear egotistical or selfish. "I just feel so uncomfortable talking about myself," they'll say. "I'd rather my work speak for itself." And that would be absolutely fine, except that most other people are not mind readers. They may look at your PowerPoint presentation or your painting or your fabulous outfit and admire it. They may even compliment you on a job well done. But many folks don't take it to the next level by accepting the compliment and pushing for more.

"Great, would you like to hear more of my ideas?"

"Awesome, would you like to see more of my paintings? They're available for purchase!"

"Thanks! I'm actually a freelance stylist. Would you like to see my portfolio?"

If you don't follow up with the people who like your stuff,

how are they going to know what you really want? How can they ever be of service to you if you don't give them the opportunity?

I didn't know that it was possible for me to do a pilot deal in which I would be a writer *and* a producer on a (hypothetical) television show. My agent told me we should push for this.

"Are you sure?" I asked. I didn't want to overreach. I thought I should appear grateful I was getting a shot at all.

I don't remember his exact words, but they added up to a more polite, professional version of "Yeah, of course we fucking should, we want that *money*! *Hell yeah!*"

We landed on a deal in which we didn't get everything we wanted, but we did get a lot of things we wanted. Why? Because we asked. Well, he asked, with my approval.

It's often fantastic to have a qualified professional advocate for you, but that's not always possible. Nor should it be. In fact, you should quite often be your own advocate. I'm happy to have my agent push for more money on a deal, or for my lawyer to negotiate appropriate legal language in a contract. I'm not an expert in those areas, and these folks have way more experience than I do. Plus, they get well compensated for their efforts, so it's not like I'm asking them to work for free.

But I don't want to work for free, either. Far from it, in fact. So when we get the chance to make a deal, I'm always going to ask for as much information as possible. How much can we plausibly ask for? What would be an implausible number? Why would that be so bizarre? Would it *actually* be nuts to name that price? I don't want to look like a madwoman who demands $5 million for a forty-five-minute speech at a small liberal arts college in the Midwest, but I also don't want to waste my fucking time.

My friends know my attitude on this kind of thing, and sometimes they'll come to me for advice.

"How much should I ask for?" they'll say.

"How much do you want?" I'll say.

"Well, I *need* . . ." they'll start to say.

"That's not what I asked," I'll say, interrupting them. "How much do you *want*?"

I did a Kickstarter for a short, funny film about body image. It was called *The Focus Group*. I asked for nine thousand dollars. A couple of people told me that was too much.

"Oh dear," they said. "That's really a lot of money for a five-minute film."

Because I knew what I was talking about and they didn't, I felt comfortable saying, "Actually, it's not a lot. We can spend as many millions as we want on a five-minute film. So nine thousand dollars is not actually that much."

And you know what? I raised more than twenty thousand dollars. Kickstarter takes fees away, and you've got to set aside some money for taxes, but before all that happened, we landed at more than twenty thousand dollars. People believed in the project, and so it gained word of mouth, and then some great press. Generous folks donated what they could. And I pushed the fuck out of the thing on Twitter, Facebook, Tumblr, and Instagram. Some people probably found it annoying. I do not care. Those people are boring. I got my money and we're going to make an awesome little film that will be way better than our original version. We can actually pay for publicity and for postproduction work, hooray! I'm also going to fulfill my promises of various Kickstarter rewards to more than five hundred donors. It's going to take a while, but I'm going to do it, dammit!

If you are confident you can make good on your promises, why not go for what you truly want? Why not take the risk of failure—or, sometimes even more scarily, the risk of success?

I know this can all be quite frightening or at least anxiety inducing. I encourage you to practice in advance of making the big ask. You can write down exactly what you wish to say and then have a friend look at it to give you notes and edits. You can take a pal out for a beer or a coffee and practice right in front of them. And of course you can practice in the mirror.

Recently, I had to do a big presentation in front of business dudes. (Calling them business dudes made me laugh, and it made me feel less nervous about making this presentation in front of them.) I was nervous and shaky at first, but I handled it with a few helpful tricks.

First, I was prepared. I was overprepared, in fact. I wrote my presentation out. I practiced it in private. I ran a little of it by some other folks in order to get their opinions. I didn't do it full out in front of anybody, but that would've been a solid move.

Second, I didn't jump right into the presentation. I spent the first few minutes chatting the folks up and talking about various pleasant things. It helped that I was genuinely interested in how their days were going. I like to know that someone with whom I'm meeting is more than just a powerful person in a nice suit. (Hint: They *always* are, but they're not always willing to show it to you. That's okay. It's their right.)

Third, I drank some water—not so much that I'd have to pee in the middle of the presentation, but enough that I didn't have a dry mouth.

Fourth, I asked *them* questions. "I've come prepared with quite a bit of material. But I really want to tailor this to you, of course. What questions can I answer for you? What are *you* interested in hearing from me?" Then, while they answered me, I drank more water. Drinking water relaxes me. Maybe instead of water, you could bring unsweetened mint tea or your favorite caffeine-free drink. (I love caffeine, but when you're nervous, it can be better to avoid it.) Take note of their questions, and make sure to hit those points during your presentation. Don't worry about sticking to script if a question comes up that wasn't in your original plan.

I hope you ask for exactly what you want, whether in the boardroom or the bedroom or in the line at McDonald's. Because you deserve all the money, all the orgasms, and all the fries. Your success does not diminish anyone else's accomplishments. In fact, if you get what you want, you're in a better position to help other people. So go on and ask, and remember the rest of us when you hit the top.

Chapter 36

DON'T BUY INTO THE **MARRIAGE MYTH**

I'm not married. I've never been married. I'm not even sure I want to *get* married. So why on earth am I writing about marriage? Well, because I know one thing and one thing only about the institution of marriage, and it's a very important thing: marriage does not make you an adult.

There is a pervasive and damaging belief in our society that in order to become a fully actualized person, one human must enter into a legal contract approved by government and/or religion. This is stuff and nonsense. It's as ridiculous as the propaganda issued forth by the wedding industrial complex, which makes gazillions of dollars a year convincing folks of all ages that they've got to "say yes to the dress" (and the heels, the corset, the lingerie, the jewelry, the hair adornments, the engagement party, the bridal shower, the bachelor party, the bachelorette party, the wedding ceremony, the reception, the music, the cake, the open bar, the fancy dinner, the morning-after brunch, the honeymoon, and so on and so forth, world without end, amen).

I like weddings. I like rituals. I like parties. I *love* dressing up and getting my hair and makeup done. But just as getting Holy Confirmation didn't make my thirteen-year-old self a good Catholic adult, nor does getting married make one a grown-up.

This can be an excellent thing. What a joy to know that just because you decided to do the big ceremony and the party with the cake and all that jazz, you still get to goof around! You don't have to lose your childlike spirit. You still get to enjoy the heck out of Disney World (that's where my brother and his lady got engaged, which seems so cool and fun to me because Mickey was nearby!). You can still be the life of the party. You can still do cartwheels and giggle at Pixar movies (before you commence weeping, obviously).

I want to be clear that the stuff I just mentioned is easily incorporated into any adult life—monogamous, polyamorous, or otherwise. But marriage, in and of itself, does not mean you're grown-up now, or suddenly mature, or that you've got your shit together. It means you had a killer party and probably your cousin got drunk and hit on another cousin (hopefully not from the same side of the family).

Here are some things that actually do represent steps toward adulthood:

1. Creating a retirement fund, even if you only put ten dollars in it to start.
2. Taking responsibility for another creature's livelihood, and all the joys and sorrows this may entail (extra points if it's a human person of any age, but I've seen some folks grow up really nicely by acquiring a dog).
3. Saying "I'm sorry" when you truly mean it. This is so difficult.

4. Framing your posters. I'm serious. I don't care if it's a Dave Matthews Band poster from 1995. You're not an adult until you put a frame on that shit. Boom! This is how it feels to be alive!
5. Houseplants. If you can take care of a houseplant, my hat is off to you. I'm still trying to master this particular aspect of adulthood.
6. Delaying gratification of any kind, because it means you understand that the eventual payoff of waiting will be better than any immediate reward could be. This is a *very* tough one. I've been working on this one since I was a kid, and I imagine I'll work on it for a long time to come. I get a teensy bit better each year.

Adulthood, then, seems to be the process by which we realize we are not the only beings in the world; that we owe care and respect to other creatures and things; and that eventually we will get old or sick or both and need resources to sustain us. Perhaps adulthood is really about grappling with and eventually facing our own mortality.

I'm not saying I'll never get married, or that I'll never do the cake or the DJ or the bouquet toss or whatever. But I do know plenty of adults who've never done it and who are perfectly happy, content, and mature. Maybe it seems obvious to you or silly, but it took me a long time to realize I didn't need a white dress to make me a grown-ass bitch. So if you share my worries, well, don't fret—we can be weird grown-ups together. And if you have been married—once or twice or thrice or whatever comes after that—well, I salute you and wish you the best.

Now remember to water those dang houseplants.

Chapter 37

TELL YOUR PARTNER WHAT YOU **LIKE** IN **BED**

Many of us are shy in the boudoir. It is not uncommon for somebody to put up with all sorts of shenanigans in the bedroom, simply because he or she is too shy to say anything to his or her partner. This is usually not the fault of said partner. In fact, if he keeps using his teeth a little when he goes down on you and you *absolutely hate it* but never say anything besides *thank you,* I'd say you're doing both of you a disservice. (I have been in this exact position before—literally and figuratively!)

I used to answer sex questions for a living, despite the fact that I knew more about the mechanics than the emotions. In retrospect, I would've spent more time talking about how sex feels on a spiritual, mental, and emotional level rather than dedicating so much time to explaining what kind of lube to use with a sensitive vagina, or how to give an excellent blowjob with less stress on your jaw, using a twisting motion with one hand. I also would've devoted less time to talking about how much I despise anal sex, which isn't actually that bad if performed correctly, and for no longer than like five seconds. I mean, hell, whatever works for you.

I've recently gained a new perspective on sex because I have friends in porn. How many friends in porn do I have? I have, at this moment, three friends in porn. I could not do what they do, if only because they are very flexible people and in excellent shape. Also, they wax everything, and I just can't handle that (except for the butt, which does not hurt). Factor in everything else about porn and I just don't think I could do it—except for the makeup. Porn makeup is basically Jersey mall makeup with a scandalous twist, and I love Jersey mall makeup.

I have learned a few things from my friends in porn, and not by watching them work. I haven't actually watched any of their stuff yet. I respect what they do, and I affirm their right to do it. I'm sure I will eventually watch their stuff, if only so I can ask, "How many times did you have to do that scene?" and "Was that fun or were you just acting like it was fun and actually you were super bored?" Right now, though, I'm still in a mental space where I'm not totally used to seeing my friends get jizzed on. What can I say? I'm old-fashioned.

One of my friends in porn told me a story about this giant studio space. It's some kind of porn empire. They do kinky stuff and they do it well, and part of the deal is that you must sign a contract indicating exactly what you are willing to do. This is as general as "I will do a girl-girl scene but not a boy-girl scene." But it gets really specific. Spanking, restraints, whipping, toys—pretty much everything you can imagine two consenting adults doing. I find this fascinating. Oh, and they have a go-to clinic in case something goes awry, like you're being fellated and a lamp falls on your head, or something. And supposedly everything is very clean, which I find reassuring.

Anyway, I've had some sex in my day but I can't say I've figured it out enough to tell you the secret to awesomeness. I think sex can be weird and fun and great and awful and sad and everything in between. There's no recipe for great sex, except that everyone involved should be an adult who consents to be there. That's the bare minimum of what is required, according to me and also according to The Law. But I do believe that just as my porn friend tells the porn empire exactly what she is willing to do, you should tell your partner exactly what you want and don't want in bed.

Of course, I don't want you to fill out a form. That's boring and weird and could involve paper cuts if things get too randy at the signing table (I assume everyone would have a signing table in their bedroom expressly for the purpose of signing such a contract). But there are ways to say, "Hey, I love what you're doing!" and "Nope." Here are some ways to tell a partner they're doing a great job:

1. Moan (in a sexy way)
2. Sigh happily
3. Say, "You're doing a great job!"
4. Say, "Holy shit, that's amazing!"
5. Say any other variation of "I like this thing that you are doing!"

Here are some ways to tell a partner they're doing a bad job or that you simply do not like what they are doing:

1. Groan (in an annoyed way)
2. Say, "Gross! I hate that!"
3. Say, "Please don't do that anymore."
4. Say, "Let's try something else instead."
5. Say, "*Stop!*"

None of this need be accompanied by shame or blame. In fact, if you and your partner can have a good laugh about mistakes, missteps, and mix-ups, your bond will likely grow even stronger.

And don't forget that this stuff is supposed to be fun. If it feels like a chore, it's probably time to reexamine some aspects of your relationship to your partner or to the concept of sex in general. And never be afraid to seek out a qualified professional from the American Association of Sexuality Educators, Counselors and Therapists.

Now go forth and get *sexxxy* in a consensual fashion that is both emotionally and physically fulfilling! Huzzah! I salute you in your quest!

Chapter 38

GRATITUDE IS UNDERRATED

I love Thanksgiving. I don't love the piles of turkey or the loads of relatives or the bullshit story about how happy American Indians helped peaceful Pilgrims and lived in harmony forevermore. I don't love the Macy's Thanksgiving Day Parade, which usually takes place on a very cold day and probably proves rather stressful for the thousands of young baton twirlers in Spandex.

What I love about Thanksgiving is the very concept embedded in its name: giving thanks. Religion can be a very complex mix of social, cultural, and spiritual values. Philosophy can be heady and difficult to parse. I've got a busy, loud brain and sometimes I like to calm things down in there and in my strange, frantic little heart. I like to keep it pretty short, sweet, and simple. For me, the best religion I've yet found can be encompassed in one simple word: gratitude.

It's challenging to go about your daily business with a constant feeling of gratitude. We have terrible days, weeks, months, even years. But if, even on an awful day, we can find just a simple little moment in which to be grateful for *something,* we may feel a tiny speck of relief.

When I was younger, I had a miscarriage. I've written about it and thought about it and talked about it, and I would never portray it as a fun experience. That would be disingenuous and also very, very bizarre. But I can remember even now, many years later, that I was grateful for a few things.

It began one night when I was in a graduate seminar at Columbia University's Teachers College. I didn't know I was pregnant. I hadn't gotten my period for a while, but I blamed it on the fact that I'd taken the morning-after pill a few months earlier, after a condom broke. I didn't have a boyfriend—this had been my one attempt at a carefree one-night stand. Anyway, sitting in my graduate seminar, I felt something snap. It was a very particular kind of snapping, nothing I'd ever felt before. And then, suddenly, came a tsunami of pain. I made my excuses and left, walking unsteadily down the hall. I collapsed in the bathroom on the floor beside the toilet, lying there for a few minutes before I gathered up the strength to keep going.

I had to take a taxi home. It was hard to walk to that taxi, but I was grateful I was able to hail one in winter weather. The cabdriver didn't understand what was going on with me, but he got me from West 120th Street down to West 92nd Street, and that was a wonderful thing. I can't imagine taking the subway or walking in such a state. Then I had to climb the front steps, which I did unsteadily. Once I got inside, I had trouble walking, so I dropped to my hands and knees and crawled for a while up the stairs. I am eternally grateful that in my indignity, when my body was taking over and doing something unfamiliar and frightening, I was not interrupted by a confused neighbor walking by. Thank goodness, I got to crawl like a crying baby in privacy.

I remember lying in bed, feeling great pain but also enormous gratitude that my roommate had Advil; that I had Xanax; and that I still possessed the little musical giraffe, Mary, I'd had since I was a baby. I played her song over and over again, and then I sang myself to sleep. I had comfortable sheets and a nice quiet room, and I was safe and warm. I was in a great deal of pain, but eventually it came in waves instead of all in one rush, and after a few hours, the waves subsided. The recovery, and the emotional processing of what happened that night, took longer. In some ways, it's still going on. I am grateful that I have this format to talk to you about it, because it is a strange and scary thing, and shedding light on it helps.

I would never tell you to be grateful in the midst of a truly traumatic experience. I would never push some Pollyanna attitude on you while you dealt with grief or loss. There are infinite horrors in this world and I believe that some things simply cannot be made better, at all, ever. But sometimes life is made a little more bearable by small blessings, little favors, tiny moments of reprieve.

I'm not a Christian, but I do recall hearing about the moment when Jesus was thirsty on the cross and a soldier wet a sponge for him to taste. It wasn't much, but it was something. It was a tiny moment of mercy in the midst of an act of great cruelty and injustice. Maybe it helped him a little bit, for a few seconds. I hope it did.

It is easy to feel gratitude for great gifts—large sums of money, perhaps, or a shiny new car, or a pricey bracelet. I once knew a woman who wanted nothing more than a very expensive white Birkin bag. Her fiancé finally got her one, and she squealed for days over how excited she was (that was a few years back; they're now in the midst of a very expensive divorce). I wonder how long that gratitude lasted before it turned into desire for the next big thing, the next fancy gift. Or maybe it simply mellowed into complacency.

It is harder to find the moments of gratitude when the subway is stuck underground for thirty minutes with a broken AC unit and you're sitting next to the stinkiest person in New York City. In this moment, you may feel enormous relief and gratitude for the empty seat down the car, or for the fact that at least your headphones are in good working order and you can listen to your favorite music while the MTA figures this one out.

In a far more serious example, you may feel gratitude that a loved one was finally able to die in peace, at home, under hospice care. You may be angry or sad that the person died, but you have a small moment in which you give thanks to the people who took good care of your loved one at the very end.

My gratitude is a daily practice. It is not constant or consistent. Sometimes it is very easy to feel gratitude. Sometimes it takes a lot of strength. My gratitude does not replace my anger, my hurt, my sadness, or my loss. It is simply something upon which I rely to help me get through life, moment by moment, piece by piece.

Chapter 39

WRITE **FAN** LETTERS

I am a fan of so many things that it's hard to name them all. I am a fan of the New York Yankees, the New York Jets, *Doctor Who,* the entire state of North Carolina, dogs, cats, the city of New York, the city of Los Angeles, people who can knit, people who can bake, people who can ride a unicycle. If you can do backflips, I think you are magic. If you can rewire any electronic device, I think you are actually a genius. Some of my favorite artists, dead and alive, include Maxfield Parrish, Jill Soloway, Diablo Cody, everyone in *The State,* David Sedaris, Nicki Minaj, Rihanna, whoever designs the spooky graveyard display at the Halloweentown store in Burbank, the great and powerful Bruce Springsteen, whoever does set design for Wes Anderson films, and on and on and on and on and on.

I am a firm believer in the idea that if you like something, you should say something. If somebody makes a beautiful thing, compliment that person! Say, "Thank you for making that beautiful thing. Because you made that beautiful thing, the world is a little bit more beautiful." Sometimes we don't get to meet the people who make the things we love the most. In this case, I think it is perfectly acceptable to write a fan letter.

Fan letters get a bad rap. People think they're old-fashioned and silly; that it's dumb to write somebody a letter when you can just tweet at them; that they make you look creepy or weird or desperate. Then there are the folks who are just too cool for school. They make a point of telling you that *they* never get starstruck and that *they* just see people as people, *maaaaaan.* Okay, Joe Cool; you stay chill and unmoved in the corner while I freak out that all three Jonas Brothers just walked into my lunch place (this happened once and my best friend Alexandra asked in wonder, "What Pandora station *is* this?").

I've had some cool mentors and helpers in my day who kindly provided assistance and/or advice specifically because I reached out via a fan letter.

Don't reach out demanding anything or even expecting a response. Just reach out. You never know.

Here is a template for a nonscary fan letter that you can send in physical or electronic mail form:

> *Dear [fill in the blank]:*
>
> *Hi! My name is [fill in the blank], and I think your work is just amazing. I wanted to tell you that the stuff you make genuinely affects my life in a very positive fashion. For example, [insert anecdote about a time something they did/said/wrote/made helped you get*

through a tough or at least boring situation]. Anyway, thanks so much for reading my letter. Keep up the great work! I believe in you.

Best wishes,
[fill in the blank]

See? That was so easy! Now all you've got to do is find some contact information for that person, or that person's publicist or professional representative. Remember to respect the boundaries of this stranger and not pester them over and over again. Just send the missive along with kind intentions and a good word and hope for the best. At worst, you wasted a half hour composing a letter and tracking down a contact email or address. At best, you may brighten up this person's day and even get something in return, such as a signed photograph, a phone call, or, if you're writing to Taylor Swift, an amazing gift box and maybe a miniature pony. That girl does fan relationships *right*.

Particularly at conventions, people will sometimes preface a very nice compliment by saying, "Ugh, I'm sorry to sound like such a fangirl." Why are you sorry to sound like a person who unabashedly and sincerely likes things? That's awesome! You're only going to make a creator happy that you dig the stuff they create. And if they don't have time for you or they're a bit brusque and standoffish, that's okay. It's really not about you. It's about where they're at in that moment. You go about your business, confident that you put some kindness out into the universe, even if it wasn't immediately reciprocated.

Of course, not everyone is going to be delighted by your presence or your adulation. I once gave an enthusiastic hug to a performer with whom I had previously worked once or twice.

She stared at me icily. Maybe I crossed a boundary by making physical contact. Maybe she didn't like me in that moment for other reasons. If I could do it again, I would just wave and say hello.

Anyway, to sum it all up: Be nice; respect boundaries; don't try to hug people unless they try to hug you first; and be enthusiastic. Keep your sincerity and your love and your kindness. Don't ever be embarrassed to like what you like. And when you really *really really* like something, drop the creator a line to say thanks. They probably worked very hard on it.

Chapter 40

ACKNOWLEDGE THAT **HAVING** A **KID** **DOESN'T** MAKE YOU AN **ADULT**

I don't have any kids at the moment. But I watch a lot of parents to learn more about this whole kid-having phenomenon that most humans seem to be so into. One time, I heard a friend say, "I think it's time to have a kid. I feel like it'll make me grow up."

Um.

Da fuq?

Having a kid doesn't make you an adult. Also, a desire for personal maturity is not a reason to bring a living being into this world. Go take an Outward Bound backpacking class or something. In the long run, it'll be cheaper and you'll probably fuck up fewer people's lives.

I've known people who were born to young moms who took excellent care of them. These young moms may have only been teens, but they took parenthood very seriously. They worked very hard to be the best parents they could be. Sure, they failed sometimes, but every parent fails at some things, regardless of age or class or level of education. From the outside peering in, it seems to me the trick is just to keep trying to be good, as often as you can. Anyway, these teen moms became grown-ups pretty damn fast.

I've also known people born to folks who were older and wealthy and educated and full of privilege but had no idea how to parent. Some of these folks acted like children themselves, throwing tantrums on a regular basis, and becoming increasingly dependent on their children for emotional and even financial resources as the children grew older. Their kids grew up very fast because they had to provide stability and support to their parents.

These people may have been parents, but they were not adults.

I don't care how old you are—if you ever feel the temptation to have a kid in order to check off some predetermined item on your bucket list; if you ever feel the urge to have a kid so that you can have a cute accessory to take to the park; if you ever feel the desire to have a kid just to help *you* "grow up"—please, for the love of all that is holy, do not have a kid. Yet. Work on yourself first. Get your shit together as best you can.

Being a parent is one of the hardest jobs out there, and if you have the privilege of deciding when to join the ranks of moms and dads, you ought to wait until you feel like an adult at least 50 percent of the time. This doesn't mean you're a dull, boring lame-o. You can still rock and roll to your heart's content. Some of the best parents I know are the ones who keep growing and changing and evolving. They still have fun and do really cool stuff. They go on adventures and take time for themselves when they can. But none of them think the child exists as a prop for an Instagram photo session. And I hope you don't, either. (Though when you *do* have a kid, I hope you Instagram all the cute stuff it does. Ooh, and dress it up in widdle bunny outfits too, please. Thank you.)

Chapter 41

A VAGINA IS NOT A TIME MACHINE

A few years back, I went through a rough phase. I can't pin it on any one thing, really. It involved a layoff, a failed relationship, and the inevitable realization that I would have to spend some time dealing with my many issues and personal flaws on my own. I decided I'd really prefer to avoid any of that messy and difficult work, and that a better idea was to focus on other things. And because I had no interest in drugs or gambling, I chose sex as my distraction.

I was in my thirties, well past the age when one can reliably blame such activities on youthful indiscretions. And I can't say it was all bad news. I had some fun. I also got involved in some bad situations that left me feeling like shit about myself, my choices, and my life in general.

I'm not slut-shaming my younger self. I believe everyone should get to express sexual desire in an open, healthy way. And I'd be proud of myself—if that's what I had done. But instead, I tried to fuck the emotional pain away. I was terrified to be alone. I suppose a lifetime of struggling with depression and anxiety had led me to believe that I was incapable of taking care of myself. Therefore, I had to stay constantly busy, constantly occupied, lest I implode.

I got my feelings hurt, and I hurt some feelings. It is impossible to fully divorce one's sexual self from one's emotional self. There will always be repercussions, and these may be good, bad, or somewhere on the spectrum in between. It is foolish indeed to imagine that one can just "fuck and run" (although that is the title of a wonderful Liz Phair song). I spent a long time wanting to be some imagined cool girl who can get it on and bounce like it means nothing. I have since realized that girl does not exist.

This doesn't mean that all sex is equally meaningful and special and glorious. It isn't. I remember one time I ended up hooking up with a much older and more famous dude right before I had plans to meet a friend for what turned out to be a date (wild times!). Immediately postcoitus with Dude #1, Dude #2 texted me. I mean *immediately*.

"Ooh, gotta go," I said to my companion. "My friend is ready."

Dude #1 looked surprised and displeased.

"Boy, you're a pro at this," he said, not nicely.

The truth was, I wasn't a pro at this. I just didn't want to be late to see my friend, and I cared more about the pal than about this fellow. But I have a habit of sometimes saying exactly what I think without remembering to check myself. This can be a great instinct for a comic or storyteller, because we end up saying hilarious things that other folks might never actually voice. It is not always the best habit in social situations, however.

Anyway, before I even realized he had just implied that I was a slut, before it registered that he had just insulted me, I said the first thing that came to my mind.

"Oh no," I said honestly, looking at him. "This is just a *you* thing." I smiled brightly and then said, "Well, thanks! Bye!" and bounced out the door.

For one moment in time, I was accidentally the cool girl I always wanted to be.

I felt like shit later, when I thought about the whole experience, but I suppose one lives and learns, right? Besides, Emily Post never wrote about that specific situation, anyway. It's not like I had a blueprint for it.

I think my displeased wealthy lover, who *of course* had a penchant for much younger gals, was probably trying to fuck his way into youthful joie de vivre. And I, for my part, was trying to relive some imagined glory days of my twenties that never actually happened. We were both wrong. Because you see, a vagina is not a time machine. Nor is a dick. Or a butthole. Or a mouth. Or— You get the idea.

Sex cannot take you back in time to a simpler era. This is why fucking your exes is rarely, if ever, a good idea. You're basically fucking the Ghosts of Orgasms Past. You need to move forward. Onward and upward, dammit! Progress waits for no one!

Here are some other things sex cannot do:

1. Sex cannot cure the common cold or any other malady except—perhaps temporarily—depression or anxiety.
2. Sex cannot make you smarter. I don't know about you, but I get immediately dumber after sex. My cognitive abilities don't return to full force until I've eaten a decent meal and taken a walk.

3. Sex cannot make you better at your job, unless your job is having sex, in which case you will probably learn a thing or two each time you do it.
4. Sex cannot make you wealthy, unless you make a tidy profit off a sex tape or license your image for blowup dolls, in which case, more power to you.
5. Sex cannot make you happy if you're not already happy. It can cheer you up for sure! It can put you in a better mood. But if you don't love the life you lead when you're not fucking somebody, your postsex glow will only be temporary.
6. Sex cannot make somebody love you if they don't already love you. Sorry, but it just doesn't work that way. Oh, it can definitely make them obsessed with you! Addicted to you, even. But love is a very different thing.

I want you to have great, fun, silly, awesome sex where you and your partner(s) crack each other up. Or maybe you cry in that beautiful way, because it's just so wonderful. But I do not want you to do as I did, and delude yourself into thinking that sex is a substitute for self-esteem. It's not. You are nobody's fuck toy (unless you're into that kind of thing) and you are nobody's door-mat (again, unless you're into that kind of thing). You're a glorious being with many interesting holes and the capacity for feeling endlessly fascinating sensations in your brain and other bits. I hope you treat yourself like the treasure you are and take good care of your emotional needs as well as your physical desires. And should a snarky famous dude ever imply that you're dirty in the bad way, feel free to tell him honestly that it's not you; it's him.

Chapter 42

ALWAYS SAY HELLO TO OLDER PEOPLE, BECAUSE THEY ARE INVISIBLE

One thing I loved very much about where I last lived in Brooklyn was the diversity of the folks in my building. They weren't just diverse in terms of skin color, income, gender, sexuality, and all that jazz—they were also diverse in terms of age. On my floor alone, we had residents from age two to age seventy-six, with a range of folks in between. On any given nice day, there would be a whole pack of toddlers playing outside while moms and grandmas and nannies looked on.

It's rare to see people of different ages voluntarily hanging out together. Young people tend to hang in packs. You're more likely to see old people walking alone, at least in New York City. Sometimes they're slower than the younger types. And I always make eye contact and say hello to the elders, because not enough people do. Mind you, I don't think I deserve a fucking medal for this; I just think it's the way things ought to be.

When someone is a young adult and perceived to be sexually available, they get plenty of attention. When they're little and cute, in the presexualized era of innocence (of course even kids are sexual beings, but you know what I mean), everybody wants to exclaim over them. And when they're babies, forget it. People love babies. Babies are life marching on, a living, breathing, diaper-shitting example of our future in motion. But old people? Old people remind us of our mortality. Old people are inclined to weakness and disease. They are often predeceased by family and friends. Sometimes they're absolutely alone in the world, and they're depressed. Maybe that's why they get ignored and dismissed. Maybe that's why some people prefer to pretend our elders don't even exist.

I'm careful to always hold doors for old women. Now, old men can be a bit tricky in this regard, as some of them have enormous pride and prefer to hold a door for a lady. I don't make a big hairy deal of holding the door for an old guy. I'll let him take over in the door-holding department if he seems to want to do that.

And good Lord, I do not use an extra-loud baby voice for older people. That shit is condescending and disrespectful. These people fought wars, or protested wars, or lost sons and daughters to wars. These people have known change and turmoil and perhaps poverty and distress. Sure, sometimes you need to shout for them to hear you, and sometimes you've got to go a bit slow for them to keep up. But don't infantilize them, please.

Now, this does not mean old people get a pass to be assholes. I don't believe that you should sit idly by and smile uncomfortably while your great-grandmother spews some homophobic or racist garbage. Challenge her old ass on her old-ass beliefs. Do her the courtesy of treating her as an equal, a person who is capable of defending her viewpoint or even, miracle of miracles, actually changing her mind. We're all adults here. Sure, some of us lived through World War II and some of us can barely remember 9/11, but we still ought to be able to have an honest conversation about important things.

When I'm old as hell, I hope I delight in hearing young people's views on the world. I'll also probably delight in telling them when I think they're totally wrong. I plan to be a jolly, badass old gal who cracks inappropriate jokes and wears weird hats. You know, like I do now, except with creakier bones. Some people will dismiss me as bananas, and I'll smile with pleasure at the freedom this affords me. And, like my one friend's grandma, I plan to have many suitors and to play them against each other mercilessly while I cackle over a glass of bourbon. And when young people pass by, I'll smile at them, happy with the knowledge that I am so much fucking smarter than they are. I hope they smile back.

Chapter 43

IDENTIFY A PERSONAL PREJUDICE AND EDUCATE IT INTO NONEXISTENCE

When I was but a wee slip of a girl, my parents put me in catechism class. We were Catholics who went to church on most Sundays, and catechism was required for me to make my First Confession, First Communion, and my eventual Confirmation. (You only get confirmed once, whereas you take communion many times, and you're supposed to go to confession a lot.)

I learned many good things from my Catholic education. The finest lesson can best be summed up as "Don't be an asshole to poor people." But I also learned some bad things, like all gay men are sick and can be cured if they choose abstinence or go through reparative therapy; lesbians aren't really having sex, because sex requires a dick; abortion is murder and women who choose abortion are bound for hell; birth control is tantamount to abortion and thus is a slightly less gross form of murder; divorce is against God's will; women who have sex before marriage are sinners; and so on and so forth. In retrospect, they could've just taught me Jesus Christ's Golden Rule and left out the rest of the hateful bullshit. It would've saved me a lot of time and self-hatred. It also would've saved me from looking down on other people who were different from me.

I got past the gay thing and the abortion thing and the birth control thing and the sex thing and the divorce thing. But well into my twenties, I still had one remaining prejudice of note: transphobia.

It wasn't like I walked around telling people that trans folks were garbage. But I held in my head the belief that trans people were mentally ill or personally defective in some way (ignore the fact that I dealt with my own mental illness and ample personal defects). I found it deeply annoying when folks in transition requested the use of them/they pronouns. It was inconvenient for me, and why should I have to accommodate their lifestyle changes? In addition, I didn't get why anyone would want to be gender-queer. It just seemed so irritating and put-on, like when you're trying to have a nice dinner at a little restaurant in New York City and a stand-up comedy show just breaks out. Awful.

This all came to a head when I worked in a place that announced that there would be a gender-neutral bathroom for folks who were transitioning or questioning. I cracked a joke about it, and my boss, who I think hated me anyway, flew into a righteous rage. He almost fired me. I'm almost certain he used it to build a case against me, but I quit soon after and went to work in the nurturing, holistic, and loving environment that is talk radio.

At first, I was mortified when he called me out. I hadn't meant any harm, and besides, it was just a joke. But then I began to think about it a bit more, and I realized that he was right.

It wasn't okay. I couldn't say exactly why it wasn't okay. I just knew it wasn't. It felt mean-spirited. So I decided to do further investigation.

First, I needed to learn the different meanings of words I'd thrown around without a clue. What was transgender? What was transvestite? What was transsexual? What did it all mean? Was it okay to use the word "tranny," and if not, why not?

I read up on the history of the transgender rights movement. This led me to my first glimpse of intersectional feminism. I didn't much like the academic and seemingly exclusionary nature of some of the rhetoric I encountered, but I found my way to more accessible writers as the years went on. One of my friends came out as trans, and he documented his journey in a way that made sense to me intellectually and that hit home for me personally.

It wasn't the job of any trans person to make me, a cis woman, feel "okay" with the existence of the Mighty Trans Other. That was on me. I needed to talk to people, real human beings, not caricatures from movies. And I needed to meet folks as one human meets another, not as some sort of anthropologist documenting the curious ways of a foreign tribe.

Basically, I needed to stop treating people like symbols and start treating people like, well, people.

I've come a very long way in this regard, and I feel good about that. Not proud, exactly—I don't think one deserves a pat on the back for realizing, "Hey, I'm a hateful fucking asshole. I should stop being one of those." But I've shown myself that people can change, if they want to. Person-to-person contact is the most important aspect of change. It is hard to look into another person's eyes and hear their honest story and still fear them, or hate them, or see them as less than you.

Some of my friends will just yell at prejudiced people. Because of my own experience, I'm more inclined to try to sit them down and have a good talk. You can't reason with everybody, and some folks are just walking shitbags. But a lot of people are like I was—comfortable with what they were taught, reluctant to change, and, when you get down to it, afraid of something different. I've realized that I used to make fun of trans people because the gender binary was so ingrained in me that I couldn't imagine living outside it. People who didn't conform with my standards of "male" and "female"—well, they freaked me out. They made me question what about me was masculine, what was feminine, and what was ultimately genderless. And I'm sure that my own ambivalence about my own bisexuality played into it in some way. When you are afraid to claim your own truth, you may become jealous of people who are unafraid to claim theirs.

Search your mind and your soul for a prejudice you retain. Then torpedo it into oblivion through the power of education. Ask questions. Search for answers. Be respectful and move forward with love in your heart. Nobody else has to know, but you'll know. And you'll be a happier person for it.

Chapter 44

LET AN ANIMAL ADOPT YOU

I was having trouble with writing a big story. Writer's block is a real and monstrous thing, and it can make you feel like a hitter in a slump. I talked to friends, all of whom had advice. I talked to a psychologist, who tried to help me get to the bottom of *why* I wasn't writing. I talked to family and I talked to strangers on the Internet. Everybody had tips and tricks. None of the help worked. I was stuck.

I'd been pestering my live-in boyfriend for months about getting a dog, and he agreed that a dog would be an awesome addition to our household. However, we both knew I needed to finish this big freelance project first. And besides, getting a dog wasn't something I wanted to take lightly. I grew up in a house with parents who repeatedly acquired and then gave away pets like unwanted toys, so it was extra important to me to be a very good and attentive pet owner. I wanted to do everything right.

On Valentine's Day weekend, my boyfriend got the idea that visiting some animal shelters might inspire me. Perhaps it would lift the writer's block that stymied my creative process. Buoyed by the promise of an eventual animal adoption, I would tear through my remaining word count and get 'er done. Then we could actually go and get a dog for real, and welcome it into our loving home.

I was game to go looking for love at the shelter. But I was adamant that we would only look at the puppies and not fall in love with any of them. We should adopt an older dog. Older dogs are adopted far less than puppies, and they deserve loving homes for their remaining years. Maybe we would even get a senior dog. Who knew?

We visited the Burbank Animal Shelter and looked at many beautiful dogs, none of whom seemed exactly right for us. Then we went over to the Glendale Humane Society, which is where we first met the puppy.

She was a little six-month-old thing, about eleven pounds, golden-haired, with a big underbite and liquid brown eyes. She was hanging out in a big cage in the front lobby when we walked in.

"This is our puppy, Annie," said the attendant.

"Oh," I said. "We don't want a puppy. We want to adopt an older dog."

We met some very nice older dogs. A hip-looking young couple came in and took Annie for a walk. They seemed to love her. They were younger than we were and they wore better jeans and sunglasses, and it was reasonable to assume they were far better suited to the puppy life. They would probably purchase very chic dog accessories and rename Annie "Lucretia" or "Bennifer" or something sophisticated like that.

We decided to go home and think about the dogs we'd met.

After all, this was just a preliminary visit meant to motivate and inspire me to get my work done.

I believe I went back to the Glendale Humane Society the very next day.

Annie was still there. I said hi and played with a few more dogs.

I went back the following day.

Annie was still there.

I met and played with a few more dogs. And every time, I said hi to Annie, who was still there in her cage.

Finally, I decided I needed to hang out with Annie. And after a few moments of holding her, I knew she was the one. When you know, you know.

I think I visited the shelter every day for a week. We applied to adopt Annie. My boyfriend didn't like the name "Annie," so we considered other options.

"Dragonbaby," I said, high off a particularly exciting *Game of Thrones* episode.

"I am not calling out the name 'Dragonbaby' in a public place," said my boyfriend.

"Why not?" I demanded. "It's awesome!" Then I imagined calling out that name in public and realized the dude was totally correct.

We kept thinking.

Finally, he said, "She looks like TV's Morley Safer."

"Do you mean TV's Andy Rooney?" I said. "Because she's got fuzzy white eyebrows."

"No," he said. "I mean TV's Morley Safer."

The more I looked at Annie, the more I realized she did, in fact, resemble the famed Canadian-born Jewish broadcaster who pissed off Lyndon Baines Johnson with early reporting on the war in Vietnam.

"Okay," I said. "Morley Safer it is. Fuck gender norms."

We did our required two-hour dog parenting course and scheduled her surgery so that she could be fixed soon. The very next day, it was time to pick up Miss Morley Safer.

My boyfriend couldn't be there, because he was at the office. I worked from home, so I had a more flexible schedule. I drove to Glendale to pick up the new love of our lives. The first thing Morley Safer did when the attendant handed her over to me was panic and claw at my T-shirt and sports bra, which resulted in a tit popping out. I saw the female attendant's eyes go wide.

"Good times," I said, putting my breast back in the proper place. "Good times."

Morley Safer cried all the way home in her little carrier. I brought her into our wall-to-wall carpeted apartment in the Valley. Then, just as I had been taught in the dog parenting class, I put her in the very nice bathroom with her kennel and toys and treats and water. Then I told her I was going out to get some supplies I'd forgotten to purchase in advance of her arrival.

She yelped and cried and I told myself to be strong. I was training her to get used to being without me. Right from the get-go, she would know she wasn't going to be some Velcro dog and I wasn't going to be some helicopter dog-parent. We were independent creatures with independent lives, and besides, I was only going to the pet supply store for like thirty minutes. No big deal.

Three hours later, I returned after spending approximately five hundred dollars on new stuff at two different pet supply stores. When I entered the apartment, it was quiet.

"I bet she's napping," I said to myself, setting my bags down. "They said most dogs nap when they're home alone."

Then it occurred to me that she might be dead. How, I wasn't sure—she had ample food and water and a very nice air-conditioned bathroom with adorable matching guest towels. (Does anybody ever use a guest towel? It seems so transgressive!) But maybe she spontaneously combusted. Did puppies do that? I really hadn't meant to be away for so long. I felt very guilty. I rushed to the bathroom and threw open the door, where I confronted a horror scene.

Oh, Morley Safer was alive, all right. Alive and delighted to see me. She was in great spirits, in fact.

She was also covered in blood.

And shit.

And urine.

And vomit.

Terrified at being left alone, Morley Safer had shat, pissed, and puked. Then she'd played in it.

And—oh yes—she'd gotten her period.

You know how happy dogs are to see their owners. We hadn't really bonded yet, but Morley Safer was psyched to see a friendly human face. And so she promptly leapt into my arms.

Imagine a furry creature covered in urine, poop, vomit, and menstrual blood, flying at your face. If you had recently adopted this creature, you might reasonably say to yourself, *This was perhaps a mistake.*

I said to myself, *This was perhaps a mistake.*

Then I went to work bathing Morley Safer (which she did *not* enjoy), after which I cleaned up the bloody/shitty/pissy/pukey paw prints that covered my previously pristine bathroom. (I didn't make it pristine. I paid somebody to make it pristine. I'm a job creator.)

I texted my fellow, who was entertained but not pleased. We had a dog in heat on our hands. I called the vet, who explained that she'd have to be kept away from other dogs for a while, particularly as she hadn't yet had all her required vaccinations. Oh, and being in heat would delay her vaccinations. Oh, and she couldn't be fixed until she'd definitely been out of heat for at least two weeks. And by the way, heat would last about two weeks.

"What do I do?" I asked. "We have wall-to-wall white carpeting."

The vet tried hard not to laugh. I could *hear* the stifled snorts.

"Buy doggie diapers," the vet said.

Resigned to spending a month essentially babysitting this dog 24/7, I put Morley Safer back in the now clean bathroom and went out to buy doggie period diapers. When I returned, she greeted me happily. She hadn't had any accidents this time.

Have you ever tried to put a diaper on a wriggling six-month-old puppy? Or any puppy, really? Or any dog of any age? They do not like it. I finally gave up and resigned myself to weeks of wiping up period blood from the bathroom floor, where she would obviously need to stay if she wouldn't keep a dog diaper on.

What the *fuck* had I gotten myself into?

Needless to say, I didn't get any writing done that day.

That night, my boyfriend came home. Morley Safer cowered when he entered. She hid behind me. I think he was a little offended. I was exhausted.

"You take her out," I said.

He did, and returned frustrated that she wouldn't poop or pee for him.

"Well, she shit all over the bathroom," I said. "I assume she's empty."

We tried to feed her, and she wouldn't eat.

"Take her out again," I said to my boyfriend. "Maybe she'll poop now. Or at least pee. Something."

What happened next was recounted to me by my shaken-up boyfriend when he returned from their outing. Apparently Morley Safer slipped out of her collar and bounded into the darkness (this was our fault, of course, for buying the wrong size). He called her by her discarded name, Annie, and she looked at him. He had a moment of deep fear. And then he remembered what they told us to do in our dog parenting class if our animal ever got loose.

"Drop to the ground and start digging like there's something very interesting down there," the instructor told us.

And that's exactly what my boyfriend did, somewhere off busy Cahuenga Boulevard in the beautiful, car-choked San Fernando Valley.

Morley Safer was immediately intrigued. Cautiously, she came over to see what it was he had found. She may have instinctively been terrified of him, but if there was some sort of dead animal to be eaten, she would put aside her reservations. And that's when he grabbed her, got the collar and leash back on, and rushed home.

All in all, it was not a banner first day. We had no one to blame but ourselves, really. Morley Safer certainly blamed us when we put her into her kennel to sleep at night. She did not sleep for hours. She cried and scratched and yelped and wailed. Thankfully, we had no neighbors on either side of us.

It's safe to say we were not particularly adept dog owners.

We put a few things together as time went on. Morley Safer was probably older than six months when we got her. In addition, Morley Safer hadn't had much contact with men while she was at the shelter. I noticed that she responded with fear whenever any men were around—friends, passersby on the street, whoever. We knew she had been dumped in the desert heat when she was barely two months old and picked up by Animal Control, so who could say what her experiences had been with guys? And besides, what female wants to hang out with a strange male when she's on her period?

Anyway, we treated her with extra loving care during her two weeks of heat. She was still skittish around my boyfriend, but that changed as time went on. When we finally got her fixed, she came home with stitches in her belly and a cone around her neck. It was time to put her to bed in the kennel she still despised, and I just couldn't do it.

"Can she sleep with us just for tonight?" I said.

"You know this means she's sleeping with us forever," my boyfriend said.

And he was right.

Today, Morley Safer is a happy, energetic ball of love.

You could say Morley Safer is a little pampered.

Morley Safer hates dancing. Morley Safer loves the park, belly rubs, sweet little kids, other dogs (though she has to dominate them, even the big pit bulls), and chicken in all forms. I am pretty sure her greatest dream in life is to murder a rodent by snapping its neck.

Because I'm an insane person, I had her DNA tested and learned that Morley Safer is part Chihuahua, part shih tzu, part toy poodle, and part greyhound. Not little Italian greyhound—regular greyhound. She is twelve pounds and nobody believes the greyhound part, but it is obviously true because science says it is true. (At the same time, I had my DNA tested. I am Druze and Palestinian and Irish and English and Finnish and Basque and Spanish and Italian and Jewish, so do with that information what you will.)

Once Morley Safer went on a six-hour plane ride with my mother and me, and I was so nervous the whole time that I cried and cried. Morley Safer was completely fine. She was also completely drugged. I probably should've taken some Klonopin before that flight. My mother says she will never fly with me and the dog ever again.

For a time, Morley Safer was featured in the real Morley Safer's Wikipedia entry. I don't know who put it in (an angel) and I don't know who edited it out (a monster).

Morley Safer is not my baby. She is a dog. She does dog things and thinks dog thoughts, probably. I love her very much but I am not inclined to dress her up or put her in a pram or do any of that creepy substitute-baby shit, because she is not a substitute baby.

That said, she is superior to most living creatures on this planet, with the exception of perhaps *your* dog and/or child.

I am fully aware that I have become one of *those* people—the dog people who will tell you every detail about their animal if you make the mistake of asking how their furry friend is doing. I do not care. Morley Safer is amazing, and everyone should know it.

What I had always heard but never believed is that your dog really ends up taking care of *you*. This is true. When I'm sad, Morley Safer stays close by me. She is a champion and fear-some security dog. She makes me fight my agoraphobia every day because if I don't take her outside regularly or go out to obtain food for her, she will suffer. I do not want Morley Safer to suffer, ever. She is sensitive and caring and loving and I wish everyone could have a Morley Safer, but I refuse to clone her because you cannot capture lightning in a bottle.

There are so many shelter dogs out there just waiting for loving owners to take good care of them. You don't have to fall totally in love with your dog the way I did—you can just like your dog, and you'll still do a fine job of taking care of him or her. You don't need a dog-walking service with a GPS tracking option, and you don't need the most expensive leashes or accessories or any of that crap. What you need is a good heart and some degree of common sense. If you put in the basic effort, your dog will return the favor a thousand times over.

Of course, at some point, you *will* need to clean up dog puke. So just take that into consideration.

Chapter 45

WALK YOUR WAY TO A **SOLUTION**

The noted raconteur John DeVore is fond of saying, "It is solved by walking." It's a famous bit of wisdom, also known in the Latin form, *Solvitur ambulando*. The saying is associated with Diogenes the Cynic, who was famous for, among other things, embarrassing Plato by talking shit during his lectures and loudly eating snacks. It's also been cited by everyone from Henry David Thoreau to Aleister Crowley, who probably yelled it while walking naked through a weird sex party.

I am agoraphobic. *Agora* is Greek for "marketplace" and *phobia* is Greek for "fear." The direct translation, then, is "fear of the marketplace." Broadly, this means fear of being in public among other people, particularly in crowds. In my specific case, it means I have sometimes turned the life of a homebody into the life of a shut-in. Even today, with all my medication and therapy, I'm more inclined to stay indoors than to go out into the world.

One can see, then, how DeVore's Latin philosophy and my Greek disorder might not exactly mesh. But I've learned a lot from him over the years, and the pleasure of a good walk is surely one of the best things he has taught me.

There is much to be said for the joy of a good hike, and I am fond of these, so long as the sun is not baking me into a pile of dust (as occurred on a few of my initial walks in the California desert). My favorite hikes happen on slightly cool, overcast days, perhaps even right after a beautiful rain. The scent of the earth rises up to meet you and you get mud on your calves, if you're really putting in the effort.

My brother once took me on a great hike in the fairy-tale woods near Hillsborough, New Jersey, where we came upon an enormous, sturdy vine hanging from a great tree. Naturally, I needed to climb it and swing around like a little kid, laughing at the unexpected joy of it all.

When I spent a semester at a castle in the Netherlands back in college, I would walk around the outer moat and look at the falling leaves. I could've contemplated the history of the restored fourteenth-century medieval castle in which I dwelt, but I think I mostly thought about boys.

Today, I have to go on walks in order to support the health and well-being of Morley Safer, the mutt who runs my life. Thankfully, Brooklyn is packed with great walks, and not just in its many beautiful parks. There are streets in Brooklyn that can take you through four centuries of history. And my other home, Los Angeles, is full of weird and winding descents and ascents into beauty and oddness.

When I am at my ancestral home in suburban New Jersey, I sometimes take long walks in my parents' neighborhood. I think about what the land was used for before it was clear-cut and turned into a housing development. I think about what it used to look like, and what I would have encountered on my walks there long ago.

Sometimes I like to do what I call a noticing walk, which is just a walk where I take care to notice things around me. Sometimes I document my walk with photographs, and sometimes with a journal. At other times, I simply walk quietly and absorb the information presented to me.

Recently, I was staying in an Airbnb in Brooklyn and going through A Sad Thing™. It was A Sad Thing of my own choosing, but still A Sad Thing nevertheless. You know how it is—sometimes you make tough decisions, and even though they may feel right at the time, they can still knock the wind out of you, not to mention the other people said decisions affect.

Anyway, I was sleeping a lot. Staying inside. Hiding from the world. I was in an Airbnb owned by an artist, and I sent my friends photos of it and they said things like, "Wow, you're definitely going to get murdered there." It was beautifully decorated and spacious but somewhat dimly lit. Also, my friends are assholes.

And one day I awoke at 3 P.M., with the afternoon light sneaking its way in through the gauzy curtains, and I thought to myself, *Get up and walk*.

It was 90 degrees and humid in Brooklyn. I did not want to get up and walk. I did not need to get up and walk.

But I got up and walked.

I got up and walked because when I don't walk, I get out of practice and descend back into my old ways. I got up and walked because when I don't walk, I miss things—the sun, the moon, the stars, the world at large. I got up and walked around the block in a pair of bicycle shorts and a ripped T-shirt that read FEMINIST, because why not?

The point is not that I saw anything life-altering (I didn't). The point is not that a nice young man talked to me about his novel. The point is not that I was perfectly all right forever and ever after I spent a half hour walking the cracked sidewalks and dodging children on Razor scooters.

The point is: I got up and walked.

The point is: I got up and walked, and it got better. Something shifted. Something small.

I remembered to breathe.

When you have a problem of some kind, it is a safe bet that a walk will do you good. If nothing else, it will get some fresh air into your lungs and some energy into your muscles. It is amazing how much even a simple walk around the block can lift you out of the fog of self-absorption and into a greater awareness of the world around you.

Chapter 46

IT'S ALWAYS TIME TO PLAY

One of the great lessons my dog, Morley Safer, has taught me is that there is no wrong time to play. Even in this very moment, as I'm trying to write this essay, she insists on bringing me her small stuffed squirrel toy and waggling her tail while she stares at me expectantly. If I ignore her, she'll occupy herself for a few seconds by shaking the squirrel very hard in an instinctive effort to snap its neck (aren't dogs adorable?). If I continue to ignore her, she has no problem putting a paw on my arm, or dropping the squirrel right on the keyboard. She's also perfectly willing to walk right on top of the keyboard and stare at me. This bitch has goals.

And honestly, if Morley Safer is in the mood to play, I should probably just play. Because I spend too much time being serious and focused, working my ass off to prove I have inherent value and am worthy of love.

Morley Safer doesn't need me to prove my worth to her. She already loves me. She just wants to play, dammit! Life is short—and hers will be shorter than mine, as I've already had thirty-five years and she'll probably only be granted about thirty-three, like Jesus—and we may as well enjoy ourselves while we're here.

You work hard. I know you do. You worry sometimes. I know you do. People who don't worry don't usually pick up books of essays on life and love and stuff. They're too busy surfing or jumping out of airplanes for fun or neglecting to apply for extra insurance on their rental car.

When you take a break from reading this very serious and academic book, do me a favor and go do something silly and stupid, just for fun. Jump in a puddle and enjoy the splash. Take a bath with a rubber duckie. Sing in the shower. Build a sand castle. Write a poem and do a dramatic recitation for your cat. Play. You've got the time. I promise the rest of your life will still be waiting for you when you finish.

Now please excuse me while I remember how to do a cartwheel. I'll likely fall on my ass and start laughing at myself, because sometimes life is hilarious even when it hurts.

Chapter 47

REALIZE **YOUR** DRESS SIZE **DOESN'T** MATTER

I used to be younger and skinny. I had a lot of skinny friends, and we would do skinny things together like try on very small outfits and wonder why people would ever let themselves get big. How did that even *happen,* anyway? It was a sad mystery.

Now I am older and wiser, and I have friends of all shapes and sizes. I am no longer skinny. My weight fluctuates depending on the time of the month, the ready availability of fried dough–based snacks on the streets of New York, the drugs I'm taking, and my emotional commitment to vegetables. When I am smaller, people who don't really "get" me will say, "Oh my God, you look *great.*" When I am bigger, those same people will say, "Oh my God, your hair looks *great.*" But my friends will straight-up tell me I look good when I look good, regardless of my dress size, and they'll mean it, too.

I have discovered that boring people measure your value by your dress size, your marital status, and whether or not you have reproduced or plan to reproduce. I don't hang around with many of these people, but I was raised steeped in this kind of culture, so I've absorbed some of it. It is a joy to unlearn these bullshit lessons.

A few years back, I began taking a medication that I've since stopped taking. My doctor prescribed it to help boost my antidepressant. I gained thirty-five pounds in three years. I am now off the medication, because it has been shown to increase one's chances of type 2 diabetes and other maladies. My family has a tendency toward type 2 diabetes anyway, and I'd prefer to avoid it if I can. But I haven't dropped the weight yet, so I'm still living in a bigger body than I was in my early thirties.

One thing that surprised me when I gained a bunch of weight was the fact that people would still talk to me. I was also shocked to discover that people still wanted to have sex with me. How odd! What a marvelous revelation! Also, I was still very smart and very pretty. Who knew? I had always been led to believe that weight gain equaled *death.* This is, in fact, not true!

I could still swim and run and do yoga, if I felt like doing those things. I could still have orgasms. I could still write books and make new friends and achieve different personal and professional goals. People still loved me, and I still loved them back. My life did not end because the number on the scale got higher.

I know many of you are scared about *that* number on the scale. You've decided that if you ever cross *that* number, you're worthless. Everything will go to shit. Well, it's not true. Your dress size does not matter (especially now that you can find cute shit in a variety of sizes thanks in part to subscription services like Gwynnie Bee).

I absolutely support you in your journey to greater health and fitness. I'm right there by your side trying to get to a better place for my mind, body, and soul. I have just learned that if that journey is fueled by self-hate, you'll never truly achieve your goals. As one friend told me, "I thought everything would be okay once I got skinny. It turns out that was a lie."

Don't wait until you lose ten or twenty or ninety pounds to start treating yourself kindly. You have to love yourself for what you are: a work in progress.

Chapter 48

THE DARKNESS IS WHERE THE GOOD STUFF STARTS

Pretty much everything awesome in my life is a result of healing, dealing with, or at least acknowledging my flaws, missteps, and failures.

When I was younger, I struggled with untreated depression, anxiety, and suicidal ideation. This led to the eventual publication of *Agorafabulous!*, my first book, a funny memoir about sad stuff. This in turn led to my getting to write another book, and getting to adapt my stories into new tales for the screen, and to speak at colleges around the country, and so on and so forth. When I was twenty-one, rocking back and forth in my bedroom, covered in my own filth, sitting beside bowls I'd filled with my own urine because I was too afraid to leave my bedroom to use the toilet—well, all this would've seemed impossible.

In addition, dealing with mental illness my whole life has made me a more compassionate person. I'm still insensitive and thick-headed sometimes, but I think I have a greater capacity for empathy than I would've had if everything in my brain worked the way it was "supposed" to. I'm less likely to dismiss someone as "crazy" just because her brain works in a unique or unusual way. I also have no shame about seeking help for mental health issues, and I like to think I've passed some of that attitude on to friends and family.

Struggling with your own sanity can give you a neat perspective on life, if you are fortunate enough to gain access to adequate treatment. I don't mean that panic attacks or recurrent violent thoughts are "fun" in any way. What I mean is that I value the good times a lot. I notice the little things and I appreciate them. I get excited about "small" things, like going to the corner store, or being able to get out of bed in the morning and ride a train or an airplane without going into a state of utter fear and breakdown.

I don't walk around in a constant, floaty state of joy. I have plenty of bad moods and ups and downs. The dark thoughts still come through. I obsess about ridiculous things. I get petty. I get jealous. I forget to be grateful for all that I've got. I complain too much and I feel sorry for myself. But here and there, now and then, I look up at the sky and get really excited that I'm alive to see it.

Years ago, I got laid off from a cool-sounding (but actually deeply stressful and awful) full-time job with benefits. Naturally, I was very worried. This was before Obamacare, so I didn't have any health insurance to cover my medication or doctor bills. I started freelancing while I searched for a full-time job with benefits. As it turns out, I was far better suited to the freelance life than to the steady-gig life. Freelancing enabled me to create my own schedule, make new contacts with media clients, grow my writing career, travel, and eventually get health insurance on my own. I was able to make more money through freelancing than I ever made through any full-time job. I got to be my own boss, and sleep late when I felt like it (which was often), and work out of coffee shops and cafés and on airplanes and in parks, and hang out with my dog all the time. Not too shabby, if you ask me.

I've derived a great deal of creative inspiration from my dark spells. I remember trying so hard to get into an MFA program right after college. I thought that was the ticket to being a writer—getting a pricey piece of paper that said I was an official woman of words, as if this would confer upon me the honor of a truly creative spirit. A wise professor said to me, "Some people should wait to get an MFA. They need to live for a while first. Otherwise, what is there to write about?" Naturally, I ignored this person and persisted in my quest. When I didn't get into any programs, I went out and lived my life, begrudgingly. Only after many years did I have the story for my first book. I can see now that the professor was right.

If I hadn't flunked half my final semester at Warren Wilson College, I wouldn't have ended up in the AmeriCorps program in the Southwest, teaching high school students. It remains, to this date, the hardest job I've ever had. But if I hadn't done that job, I wouldn't be able to repeat the phrase that has so often given me comfort in the years since: "No matter how hard this particular gig is, *I am not responsible for the welfare of children.* And that makes all the difference." Then I smile and bang out the spreadsheet or the presentation or the treatment or the joke or the proposal or the pitch.

Also, if I'd graduated on time, I wouldn't have gotten to take a really great health class at New Mexico State University to fulfill the final four credits of my degree. It was truly one of the best classes I ever took in college.

A friend once taught me a more extreme version of the "welfare of children" lesson. I was obsessing over some problem at work and he said, "Ask yourself, 'If I don't do this perfectly, will children die?' If the answer is no, you'll be just fine." I recognize that this is not helpful for pediatricians and child-care workers, but for the rest of us, it's great!

If I'd been popular and pretty in elementary school and in middle school, I don't know that I would have developed such a rich inner life. The world of my imagination was a safe and wonderful refuge from my constant feelings of isolation and inadequacy. To this day, I'll sometimes take an hour or two by myself to "have imaginings," which just means I lie down and build new worlds in my mind. There's no specific purpose to it—no end goal, no metric by which to measure my productivity. It's simply a practice in which I've engaged since I was very small.

I could go on and on, but books are not limitless things. We have to stop at some point. And we're getting closer to the end of this journey we've taken together. We're not quite there yet, but we're close. So I shall leave you for the moment with this bit of advice: Think of all the ways in which you've failed, messed up, fallen short, or been embarrassed, abandoned, rejected. Can you take any of the raw stuff of those sorrows and build something new and beautiful out of them? Here's another way to look at it: can the story of your past troubles help somebody else lead a better life? You don't have to be an altruistic individual to derive comfort and satisfaction from helping others avoid your own mistakes or missteps.

I'm not asking you to *do* anything right away. Just give it a thought. Then set it aside and let it percolate for a while. Tomorrow, or next week, or next month, or next year, it may just lead you to surprisingly great results.

Chapter 49

YOUR NORMAL **IS NOT** EVERYBODY **ELSE'S NORMAL**

Recently, in the vast depths of the glorious oasis of reason and thoughtful commentary that is Facebook, some strangers were talking about a celebrity who had been accused of child molestation. Most people were, if not convinced that he was guilty, at least convinced that the very concept of child molestation was a bad, bad, bad, bad thing.

And then there was this one person.

(There's always one, right?)

She wrote something like this: "I mean, so what if he touched his sister a little? Who hasn't been touched by their older brother? That's how little boys learn about sex. You just grow up and get the fuck over it."

Um.

Uh.

Er.

Oh, dear.

Let's set aside the fact that this girl may have some upsetting trauma in her past. (Note: I am not one of the alarmists who consider all expressions of childhood sexuality to be taboo. But something felt off about this gal's remark.) Let's focus on the fact that she made a very dangerous assumption: everybody else had the exact same childhood she did.

It is impossible to know the totality of someone else's life experience. What is possible is the recognition that said life experience differs from yours. I don't care if you're identical twins raised in the same household who attended the same schools and then married a pair of identical twins; you and your twin have different life experiences. Never make the mistake of assuming you know exactly what another person went through. You can empathize, certainly, but you can't know what it was like to be in their shoes.

Growing up in a relatively sheltered suburban/rural environment, I used to assume that everybody else had the same relationships to friends, family, and community as I did. Good Lord, was I wrong. We all walk around in these human bodies, and we don't have the same eyes, the same ears, the same noses, the same anything. Everybody perceives the world a little bit differently. It's overwhelming to contemplate and difficult to accept, but this is how it is.

This lesson was brought home to me once again very recently. I was up late working on this very book, and I had a familiar case of what I always called "the rumbly tumblies." I had never actually asked anyone else if they had the rumbly tumblies. I just assumed everybody did.

Beginning when I was very small, I noticed that sometimes my heart would seem to thump around in my chest. It was like my heart was skipping a beat, then doing an extra little shimmy and shake in my chest to catch up. I called it the rumbly tumblies because it felt like something in my chest was rumbling and tumbling. It never hurt and it never caused more than a few seconds of alarm. I'd feel it do its thing, and then I'd feel a sudden shot of adrenaline from my friendly and overworked adrenal glands. After a moment of panic, everything would settle right down again and I'd go on with my life.

This happened maybe once a month for my entire life. Then I started talking about it on Twitter the other night, like, "Hey, isn't it funny when that happens?" And I got a resounding response of "What the fuck are you talking about? Please go to a doctor immediately."

"You mean you don't get this, too?" I asked in wonder.

"No," said Twitter. "Nope."

"Oh," I said.

The next day, I ran it by my boyfriend.

"Have you ever brought this up to a doctor?" he asked, his expression tightening.

"No," I said. "Isn't that weird? I thought it was normal."

"It is not normal," he said.

Well, as it turns out, he and the Internet were right! It's not normal! Who knew? (Everybody else, apparently.) But because I had automatically assumed that everyone's experience was the same as mine, I had dismissed what could've been a significant problem in my life. (I'm fine, by the way. It's most likely one of three things, none of which is fatal, all of which can be exacerbated by stress and high caffeine intake. Yes, I'm going to the doctor.)

Think about your own life, your own experience. What have you always accepted as absolutely normal? Now, with the benefit of hindsight and perspective, what do you think might be odd or unusual? Think about physical sensations, emotional sensations, childhood experiences. Talk to your friends about these things. You may find, as I did, that you deserve a little extra help and more care than you thought necessary. This is not necessarily a bad thing! You also might find some folks who go, "Oh man, I thought I was the only one who went through that. You did, too?" And then the world will feel a little smaller and cozier, and everyone will be a little bit healthier and happier, all because you decided to open up about your own personal case of the rumbly tumblies.

Chapter 50

THIS TOO SHALL **PASS**

Are you happy?

Are you sad?

Are you somewhere in between?

This, too, shall pass.

What am I talking about?

I'm talking about everything.

Everything passes. All of it. One day this book will be dust and so will you and so will I. That's terrifying and wonderfully comforting.

Every breath will pass. Every mood state will pass. You know this moment? This very moment, right now?

Well, it's gone.

We're on to a new moment.

And here's another one.

And here's another one.

It all changes—the good, the bad, and everything else.

When you get caught—when you get stuck—when you get frightened or worried or filled with despair, please just remember: it's going to pass.

This is the only thing that is always, always, always true.

Chapter 51

ALWAYS CELEBRATE RAINBOWS

Rainbows are awesome miracles from the heavens above. Yes, I know they're actually just refracted light or something, but I don't give a fuck. Rainbows are amazing and I always make a huge deal out of them. There are probably not actually diminutive Irishmen granting wishes at the end of the rainbow, but we can't know for sure, can we?

Anyone who doesn't get excited over rainbows, or at least smile a little bit at the sight of one—well, that person is a dried-up raisin of a human. Do you want to be a dried-up raisin? No. You want to be a luscious, full-bodied, delicious grape. If grapes could talk, they'd talk about rainbows. They would also request to not be made into wine, probably.

Never lose that childlike glee over seeing a rainbow. Point 'em out. Ask people, "Did you see the rainbow?" If they didn't, tell them where to find it. Why would you not want everybody to know that? *The sky is smiling at you.* Celebrate that shit. It's fucking beautiful.

Chapter 52

LOOK IN THE MIRROR AND SAY "I LOVE YOU"

Whenever I catch sight of my reflection in a mirror, I say something—aloud or silently.

"I love you."

Not "You're perfect."

Not "You're infallible."

Not "You're the best person ever born in this universe or any other."

Just, simply, "I love you."

Sometimes I don't really feel it. Sometimes I'm mad at myself or deeply ashamed or just plain depressed. Sometimes I'm full of self-hatred. Sometimes I want to kill myself.

I still say it.

"I love you."

When you tell a child something often enough and with enough apparent conviction, she will believe it.

Think about the things your parents told you—how smart

you were or weren't; how beautiful you were or weren't; how talented you were or weren't.

How loved you were or weren't.

Your parents may be absent or gone forever. They may remain a part of your life, for good or for bad. But you're old enough to tell yourself the truth now, and the truth is that on some level, somewhere inside you, there is love.

"I love you."

No one has to know you do it. No one has to hear you say it.

But you'll know.

And one day, if you do it enough, you will believe it.

I wish you the best. I wish you love. And I wish you a wonderful life.

"I love you."

ACKNOWLEDGMENTS

This is my favorite part to write. I know it's long. You'll deal.

Thanks to Cassie Jones, an awesome editor—this is our second book together! You are a delightful and very pretty human being and I am pleased to know you and call you a friend. Thank you for your patience, insight, and good humor. You are a real artist with a day job, where you are an artist, during the day, at your job.

Thanks to my bloodthirsty, sharklike literary agent, Scott Mendel, and his scheming assistant, Elizabeth Dabbelt, as well as my agents at ICM—Doug Johnson, Melissa Orton, and Josh Pearl—and my agent at Keppler Speakers, Sean Lawton. Thanks to their respective assistants, too. Thank you to LaWonne Tolson at Keppler for always getting my travel done and being so helpful. Shout-out to wee babies Clive Johnson, Mabel Star Lawton, and Elijah Sal Pearl, born (and likely conceived, actually) while this book was under way!

Thank you to two-time James Beard Award–winning writer and nonstop creative force John DeVore and our wee baby dog from the Glendale Humane Society, Morley Safer. I love you both. Thank you to Lazé Dunn in Brooklyn and Tiffany Lee in Los Angeles.

Thank you to the team at William Morrow who's responsible for my book, including Kara Zauberman, Kenneth Hoffman, Liate Stehlik, Lynn Grady, Jennifer Hart, Amelia Wood, Joseph Papa, Ivy McFadden, Diahann Sturge, and Elizabeth Hanks. You all deserve tons of credit for your hard work.

Thank you very much to the hardworking folks at all the places where I wrote this book (besides my apartment and my parents' house).

- The General Greene in Fort Greene, Brooklyn (excellent ice cream)
- Putnam's Pub in Clinton Hill, Brooklyn (really good fried chicken)
- Los Angeles International Airport, Terminal 3 (enjoy the Virgin America lounge)
- The Tangerine Hotel in Toluca Lake, Los Angeles (comfortable bed)
- Hotel Amarano in Toluca Lake, Los Angeles (*really* comfortable bed)
- The Georgian Hotel in Santa Monica, California (great atmosphere)
- The Abode of Audra Williams, Toronto, Ontario, Canada (so exotic!)
- Saving Gigi, Toronto, Ontario, Canada (excellent seating options)
- The Abode of Adam Thabo, Brooklyn (cool dried bones)

- The Pink Palace, Los Angeles (hot babes)
- The Abode of Steve and Elaine, New Jersey (nice Squatty Potties)
- My Parents' House, New Jersey (nice seashell-themed bathroom)

The official airline of *Real Artists Have Day Jobs* is Virgin America. Thank you for your gummi snacks, your half a peanut-butter-and-jelly sandwich, your comfortable seats, and your disco lighting. Your in-flight safety video is groundbreaking and stunning. Please get rid of your seat-to-seat messaging system. It is your only flaw and creeps me out. No, I do not want to chat with "the person in 16C," unless that person is Richard Branson, who seems wonderful.

I'd like to publicly apologize to Paul Rudd for convincing America in October 2014 via the hashtag #PaulRuddSavesLives that he was present in a viral video of a bunch of airport denizens tackling a nasty homophobe. Wow, business executive Ben Kravit of Dallas, Texas, you *really* looked like Paul Rudd for a second there. Thank you to major international media for running my unverified, speculative story. Thank you to *Ant-Man* director Peyton Reed for kindly and gently acknowledging my embarrassment whilst you were in production in Atlanta, and for directing those amazing episodes of the UCB TV series in 1998 and '99.

I'd also like to publicly apologize to the owner of #XRayCat for any stress or trouble that my live-tweeting your putting your cat through the X-ray machine at LAX may have caused you in July 2015. I was just so amazed when the TSA lady started gasping, "You *put* your *cat* through the X-ray machine?!?" I know it was an innocent mistake, and I wish you the best. Thank you to major international media for running this actually true story. Ultimately, we are all #XRayCat.

Some artists and doers (some friends, some acquaintances, some total strangers) who inspired me during the creation of this book: my beautiful Kickstarter backers who made *The Focus Group* (2015) and This Tour Is So Gay (2014–15) happen; yoga witch Rachel Perry Mason; creative genius and my forever comedy wife Diana Saez; good Christian woman Gretchen Bauer Stanford and her gentleman husband, Tim; Jon and Eddie; Jill Soloway, Rebecca Odes, and Keely Marina Weiss for Wifey; Adrian Todd Zuniga for Literary Death Match; Bobcat Goldthwait for *Call Me Lucky;* Lena Dunham for sending me the alluring sexytime Lonely Lingerie underpants I am currently wearing; Barry Crimmins (who probably feels weird about being named right after the underpants comment); Hayley Rosenblum and Maris Kreizman at Kickstarter; Debbie Liebling; Diablo Cody; Mason Novick; Heather Fink; Allegra "Mrs. Harris if you're nasty" Riggio; the Pussy Posse; Cunt Club; Josh Gondelman; Bob Saget; John Leguizamo; Marielle Heller for *The Diary of a Teenage Girl*; swimspirational video star Wylie for the backfloat; Roxane Gay for encouraging me to do some tattoo rehab; Corinne Kingsbury; Lil' Baby Aidy Bryant; Taylor Swift for being fucking amazing; Michael Ian Black; Rihanna (who is always listed immediately after Michael Ian Black in my acknowledgments, as per my contract); Amy Poehler; the folks at Dear Kate underpants; Marni van Dyk and Molly McGlynn for *I Am Not a Weird Person*; Myq Kaplan; Mos Def and Talib Kweli for their 1998 debut album; Ben Stiller for understanding the emotional power of *Jesus Christ Superstar*; Maria from GentleWhisperingASMR, because you are magical; Rebecca Trent; Caitlin Stasey; Lucas Neff; Tom Calderone; Steve Basilone; Todd Strauss-Schulson; Jake Fogelnest; and anybody who made art or coffee that helped me get this book done. That includes you, Lauren Brown.

Thanks to actress-writer-badass Amanda Deibert Staggs for being there for me when I was in a tough spot late one night.

A final shout-out to Cora and Juliette Baxley, Lilah and Neva Mason, Vivienne Diane Staggs, and Penelope Weston. May you grow up in a world where all your work is appreciated, wanted, and loved. And may you be compensated more than seventy-seven cents on the fucking dollar.

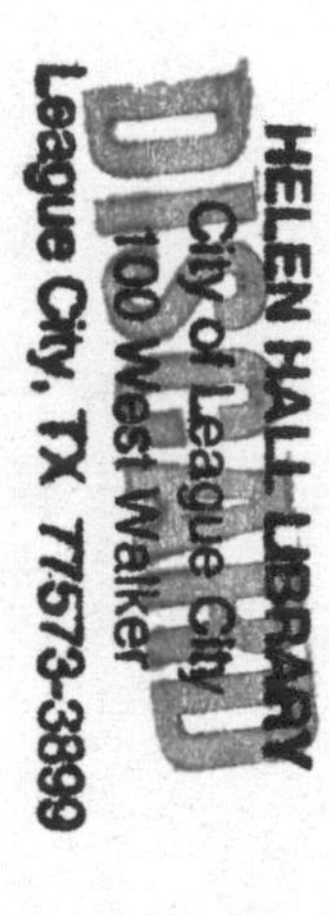